CORPSE ROAD

A Montague and Strong Detective Agency Novel

ORLANDO A. SANCHEZ

BITTEN PEACHES
PUBLISHING

ABOUT THE STORY

Killing an enemy once is difficult...having to kill them twice is just unfair.

Monty's recent shift in power after using the First Elder Rune has awakened old enemies.

Enemies who were once dead have been cursed to roam the earth again...with one purpose.

Destroy Tristan Montague and Simon Strong.

Now, together with the help of Simon and his uncle Dex, Monty must discover how the dead have risen—and, more importantly, how to return them to their graves.

In order to succeed, they must locate a powerful necromancer rumored to be dead for centuries.

When it comes to old necromancers, the dead have a tendency to wander the night, and the rumors of their death may be exaggerated.

If Monty and Simon don't reverse the curse in time, they may soon join the undead hunting them.

"Oderint dum metuant."
(Let them hate, as long as they fear.)
-*Lucius Accius*

DEDICATION

My humblest and deepest thanks for teaching me this, Terry:

"Do you not know that a man is not dead while his name is still spoken?"

-Sir Terry Pratchett

ONE

Battle-form training.

More like battle-form failing.

The storm was making this impossible.

If it was just rain, this would be doable. I could deal with fighting in the rain. It was the combination of rain and wind that made this difficult. I looked up into the sky as the wind threatened to rip me off the roof, and let out a low growl of disgust.

At this point, the rain was actually coming at me sideways, forcing me to turn my face away from the wind. My clothes, my *everything*, were soaked.

I looked down at my hellhound, who looked about as happy as I felt, and shook off some of the water from my face. He gave off a low rumble as he withstood the rain, giving me a massive dose of side-eye.

"Hey, don't give me that look," I said, futilely removing some of the water from his massive face as thunder crashed in the distance. "This *training* wasn't my idea. Blame Dex."

<Will there be meat after this? I'm hungry and wet. I don't like being hungry and wet.>

<First of all, you're always hungry. As for being wet, we can't help it in this storm. We may as well be training in the ocean.>

<I don't want to train in the ocean. Can we go to the place after the training? The old man who smells like home always has good meat for me.>

<I'll see what I can do. At the very least, I'm sure the Bear has some meat. I'll ask her to share some with you.>

<I like her. She smells nice.>

<Sure she does. She's probably the reason we're standing in this storm right now?>

I glanced over at the large werebear standing off to the side, keeping dry under the canopy on the roof. She waved at me as I glared at her.

<She made it wet?>

<Not her, but I have a feeling that hammer of hers had something to do with it.>

<I still like her. She gives me good meat when we visit.>

<You would. Are you rested? This break isn't going to last forever.>

<I'm not tired. She said we were taking a break for you. You still don't understand our battle form.>

<She did say that, didn't she? Fine. We'll try it again when she attacks. This time, we make it work.>

<I can make it work every time.>

<I'm sensing some judgment here. I've never had a battle form, you know. Some of us aren't hellhounds.>

<If you would eat more meat, you would be stronger. Then you could use our battle form every time.>

<I'll get right on a new diet. In the meantime, we have to make this work or we'll be out here all night. Who trains like this at night?>

<We do. I'm ready, bondmate. Let's show her how mighty I am.>

<How mighty you are?>

<You will become mighty...when you get stronger. Right now, I will be mighty for both of us.>

<Of course you will. Let's do this.>

Peaches rumbled again in response, hunkering down against the unrelenting wind and rain as he looked across at our target.

We had been at this "training" for close to an hour.

Our opponent appeared to be enjoying herself. I made a mental note to devise some sort of revenge thank you for Dex who had been the one to suggest this specialized training session. Maybe I could have Peaches chomp on one of his legs.

Knowing Dex, though, he would just ply my ever-voracious hellhound with premium sausage and ruin my plan. For a nearly indestructible and unstoppable hellhound of destruction, he was easy to distract if you knew the right strategy.

I stretched my back and twisted out some of the kinks.

My body was feeling the wear, even if it had been repairing itself. My curse had kept me alive from a few close calls and near misses.

Her last attack, a bare-knuckle fist to my face, nearly rearranged my jaw to the back of my head. I rubbed my face as my body flushed with heat and dealt with the damage.

"There is no block," Nan said, calling out from across the roof with a wide smile as she stood in the downpour opposite us. "Have you not learned this yet?"

"My face disagrees," I said, still rubbing my jaw as Nan hefted her weapon while keeping her gaze fixed on me. "Are you sure Dex agreed to this?"

Still smiling, she gave me a slow nod.

"*Horrendous*," she said. "Oh, and *subpar*. Those were *some* of the words he used to assess your performance in your battle against Keeper Gault. He said you should have died several times over."

"So nice of him to cheer me up that way," I said. "I can always count on a mage to lift my morale."

"That old man doesn't do nice," she said. "He said some other, more colorful things. That man knows curses I've never even heard—and I'm a seasoned valkyrie. We *know* curses. We even invented some of them. Would you like the full assessment?"

"Pass," I said, raising a hand. "My ego can only take so much encouragement. I get the general message—I should've done better. Is that why he sent you and arranged all this?"

"Aye," she said, her voice serious, but her smile mischievous. "Said he had matters to attend to at the school, and didn't want us renovating the grounds...again. Something about having you and Tristan there being too much potential damage at once."

"He kept Monty at the school and sent me here? Really?"

"Tristan is facing the Chooser of the Slain," she said with a slight shudder. "You get me. All things considered, I'd say you got the better end of that arrangement. As far as training halls go"—she looked around the roof—"this is one of the better ones I have had the privilege of doing battle in. Thank you, Favored of Ukko, for your hospitality."

"You're welcome," Ursula said from where she stood, off to the side. "At least some people understand the word gratitude."

"I'm supposed to be grateful that you loaned us your roof so I can get pounded on?" I asked in disbelief. "You must be joking."

"You should be grateful that you can test the outer limits of your newfound ability here, on my training floor, and not while facing someone or something that wants to rip your face off, only to discover you can't access this battle form when you need it the most."

She had a valid point.

I bowed in her direction, which she returned.

"Thank you for the privilege of training on your floor," I said. "The more we bleed in training—"

"The less we bleed in battle," she finished. "Not the exact quote, but it works *if* you learn the lessons."

I nodded and took in my surroundings.

We were on the roof of the DAMNED Headquarters.

I looked around the roof of the renovated and modified carriage house. It appeared to be more a contained training area than a normal roof. High walls, which I was certain violated some kind of air rights code, prevented neighbors from easy viewing.

The roof was divided into several sections, and all the equipment was weatherproof. Apparently, Ursula enjoyed training outside just as much as she did training indoors.

Must've been a bear thing.

Despite the fully equipped training facility inside the building, Nan suggested we conduct the battle form training on the roof, supposedly to 'get some fresh air' while we trained.

The indoor training space on the bottom level was designed to withstand use from Ursula, a werebear, who conveniently was continuing to stand just inside the covered patio and out of the torrential downpour I was still being subjected to.

I shot her another look, as lightning raced across the sky.

"Well, that explains why we're here," I said. "What it doesn't explain is the monsoon I'm currently standing in. Any thoughts on that, Bear? You have something to do with our wonderful training weather?"

"Perhaps," Ursula said with a small chuckle. "Ask your trainer."

Nan laughed.

"You must be able to fight in every condition and on any terrain," Nan said. "You must be able to adapt to every eventuality. You and your mighty hound must be able to fight as one."

"And you anticipate us facing our next enemy in a hurricane?"

"I anticipate you facing your next enemy wherever you need to—be that a hurricane or the depths of hell itself," she said, the smile across her lips turning into something darker and scarier. "Wherever that battle occurs, you two must be ready. That is the task I was given, and you *will* be ready...or you will die in the training."

"I'm not a valkyrie, you know," I said, sliding into a defensive stance and holding Ebonsoul across my body as Peaches entered tear-and-shred mode. "I'm not applying for the Midnight Echelon."

"I know," she said, her voice somber as she gazed at her axe. "Did you know that every member of the Echelon does battle under one truth?"

"What? Pain is part of the process?" I asked. "If you're not bleeding, you're not training hard enough?"

"Both true, but no," she said. "We have a simple saying: *unus exercitus*. Do you know what that means?"

I nodded.

"My Latin is rusty, but that one is easy: *one person is an army*."

She nodded in response.

"Do you know why that is the driving philosophy of the Midnight Echelon?"

"Each of you is powerful enough to hold off an army?"

"No," she said with a shake of her head, "though that's probably true. It is to remind us that no one is coming. No one is going to rescue you, and no one is coming to your aid. It doesn't matter how many stand against you. *Unus exercitus.*"

"Even if that means falling in battle?"

"If my death can save the lives of my sisters, then it is an honorable death," she said without hesitation. "Do you understand this concept—an honorable death?"

I nodded again.

"I do," I said. "Not a concept I actively pursue—you know, my enjoying life and all—but I do understand and accept it, yes."

She smiled again and cracked her neck, never taking her eyes off me.

"Good," she said, lifting up Stormchaser, her double-bladed axe, and rolling her shoulders. "Tonight, our conversation will be about death...yours."

She ran at me.

TWO

The natural air of menace that hung around Nan like a concentrated threat-cloud reached me before she did. It was most likely due to her axe Stormchaser the menacing double-headed axe headed my way.

"I bring you clarity of mind and purpose, Strong," she said, as she closed on me. "I gift these to you in the purest form possible—pain and death."

"I'm guessing declining these gifts is out of the question?"

"It would be rude to decline them," she said, swinging her axe down at my head. "There is a no-return policy."

Who knew valkyries had a sense of humor? Twisted and dark, I admit, but still there.

I raised Ebonsoul blocking her downward strike as Peaches blinked out and reappeared near her neck. Her initial blow reverberated throughout my entire body.

She laughed at his attempt and slapped him away with one hand, while she bore down on me with the axe in the other.

Peaches flew across the roof and crashed into one of the walls, shattering it with the impact of his body. He rolled off the wall and landed solidly on his paws, cratering the floor.

He shook his body and growled.

"Yes, Mighty One, show me your power! More importantly, show your bondmate how it's done. Come! Attack me!"

There was no way to face her toe-to-toe. She was too strong. I had a better chance of wrestling a charging rhino into the ground, than I had stopping Nan head-on.

I deflected the axe into the floor by angling Ebonsoul and rotating around her attack. As the axe slammed into the floor, the blade burying itself into the wood, she released it and backhanded me across my chest.

It would have been gentler to be hit by a truck doing sixty.

I bounced across the wet floor and rolled to my feet as heat flushed my body. If I hadn't been blocking with Ebonsoul, she would've caved my chest in with that strike.

"There will be no quarter given," she said, her voice low and dangerous, as she pulled Stormchaser from the floor. "You either execute the battle form, or I execute you."

"None asked," I said, circling around the large floor and beckoning her closer with a hand. "Bring it."

Her black combat armor gleamed in the rain as black energy trailed Stormchaser every time she moved it. I could tell from her intent those weren't just empty words. If I didn't fight as if my life depended on it, I would find out how quickly her axe could cut me out of existence.

"Use all of your weapons, Strong, save the gun," she said, stepping toward me. "Your gun can be stripped, dropped, or lost. Your blade is a part of you, along with whatever cast you know. Those you cannot lose. Those cannot be taken."

"Cast? My cast won't do anything to you," I said. "I don't command the power of a mage."

"You don't need to," she replied. "You're a bondmate to a hellhound. Command *that* power."

<Let's do this, boy.>
<Stand still. This will hurt.>
<Not as much as that axe will if we don't pull this off.>
<Concentrate. We are bondmates. We are one.>

My arms burned as I felt him next to me. He stepped close and I buried a hand in the scruff of his neck. He unleashed a low growl, which thundered across the floor.

Nan smiled when she heard it and nodded in our direction.

"Yes," she said, with a wide smile. "Unleash the beast."

I felt a concentration of heat in my stomach as Peaches' presence grew beside me. He didn't go XL, but somewhere in between XL and his normal size.

The top of his head was level with mine and his fur went from black to a deep blue-black with a metallic sheen. The runes on his flanks blazed with red and violet energy—more red than violet—and matched the runes that formed on my arms.

The pain became excruciating, and my screams joined Peaches' howls, as it overtook me. I saw the muscles form on his body as we both transformed. His shoulders spread out as he grew, and my skin became denser and heavier.

The agony kicked it up a notch as Nan swung her axe at me. I grimaced at the sensation as I brought up Ebonsoul and parried her axe. It was easier this time, similar to stopping a bus rather than a stampeding elephant bent on crushing me to dust.

Orethe's words blazed in my memory: *It's only pain, Simon. You should be intimately acquainted with it by now.*

I was acquainted, all right. Didn't mean I liked it, but the sensation was familiar.

I laughed to myself as the pain cocooned around my body and squeezed mercilessly. For a brief second, my vision tunneled in and then I felt a sensation of energy explode in my eyes.

This is new.

If I had stared into the sun for ten minutes straight, it would be more pleasant than this new sensation of power in my eyes, forming a haze of violet and red energy formed around them.

She swung Stormchaser, which I ducked. She continued her swing, turning the axe sideways as she swung over my head and into Peaches' flank, hitting him with the flat of the blades.

The impact was staggering.

She launched him off the side of the roof, and into the night. He blinked out of sight as she dropped her axe and connected a spinning back-fist with my head.

All the red and violet energy instantly disappeared from my vision as her fist connected with my head. Her attack spun me around and into a kick which launched me over the edge of the roof.

"We'll have none of that from you," she said, as I flew off the roof. "Good try, though. Enjoy your flight."

For a moment, I couldn't believe she had kicked me off the building. My disbelief quickly transformed from shock to anger as I reached out to my hellhound.

<Here, boy! We need to attack her now while her axe is dropped.>

Peaches blinked out again and reappeared with his powerful jaws around my arm. He blinked out again several times in succession and landed on the roof behind Nan.

My stomach did a few somersaults when we arrived, as I nearly ejected my early dinner while I stumbled to the side. Peaches barked at Nan, unleashing a shockwave that drove her to the edge of the roof. More importantly, it drove her away from Stormchaser.

My body flushed with more heat than I had ever experienced as I ran at her. She met my approach with a fist to my head. I dodged to the side as Peaches flanked her and rushed her side.

She stopped him cold with an outstretched arm and greeted my evasion with a kick designed to break ribs. Ebonsoul fell from my hand and vanished into silver mist. I brought my arm down and protected my side as she unleashed an elbow at my head.

I ducked under the elbow strike and punched at her knee, aiming to shatter it.

Had I connected, this fight would've ended then and there, but she had other ideas.

She cut the knee-shattering plan short by driving her knee into my face which erupted with an explosion of pain. I fell back as blood poured from my nose. Peaches clamped his jaw around one of her arms, and she smiled as he began to shake.

She was about to punch him away when I dove forward and jumped in the way, blocking the strike and taking the blow on my side. This time she did manage to break my ribs, while dislodging her arm from his jaw. A white-hot lance of pain shot up my side, stealing my breath away as I drove an elbow into her temple.

Much to my surprise, I managed to connect and whip her head around to one side as my newly broken ribs screamed at me with the sudden movement.

The shock of the blow sent her back several steps and I bought us some distance from her punishment. Peaches rolled to the side and jumped up in the air, blinking out as he did so.

I hissed through the pain and formed Ebonsoul as I ran at her again. This time we were approaching from different angles—Peaches from above and me from the side.

We had her trapped.

I saw the red glow of energy form around Peaches' eyes. He was going to unleash a baleful glare at her.

She was done.

THREE

I was wrong.

So wrong.

She outstretched an arm, forming Stormchaser as twin beams of energy shot out from Peaches' eyes, heading for her face. Using her axe, she deflected the baleful glare away from her—right into my chest.

The twin beams punched into me, knocking across the wet floor of the roof and onto my back. Nan sidestepped and dodged Peaches' pounce, kicking him while he was still in mid-air.

He flew off the side of the roof and into the night at speed. She didn't give him a second glance as she whirled around and raced at me, all the while swinging her axe in a circle beside her.

I saw the plan.

It wasn't going to be pretty if she connected.

She would bury the axe in my chest as soon as she caught up to me. I needed to prevent that axe from ending up there, and I had to do it alone.

Peaches was currently mid-flight, and she was closing.

I absorbed Ebonsoul and drove my fingers into the wooden floor of the roof, cutting grooves in the wood with my fingers. My action pulled my body to one side as I twisted away from her, changing the trajectory of my slide.

She made to turn but slipped on the wet floor as she course-corrected. It wasn't much of a slip, but it was enough to give me a few seconds to catch my breath.

"*Ignis vitae!*" I yelled, pointing one arm at her. She didn't have enough time to react as an intertwined violet, gold, and black beam of energy seared through the air, turning the rain to steam as it raced at her.

The beam caught her in the side and knocked her sideways as Peaches blinked in with a growl and rammed her with his enormous head. She went sailing off the side of the roof as he blinked out again.

I took a moment to catch my breath and hunched over, my hands on my knees as I gasped. We had managed to stop her attack and get her off the roof.

For half a second, I relished the thought we had launched her off the roof and into the night. Then, that small voice in the back of my brain kicked me in the shin, getting my attention.

She's a valkyrie.

So what? I answered with satisfaction. *We sent her flying off the roof. Did you see her? She took off.*

Exactly. You sent her...flying. You do recall that valkyries have wings?

Oh, shit.

Duck?

Too late, I felt the impact crash into my back and shove me forward with force. It would have whiplashed my neck and shattered my spine, if my body hadn't become denser from the battle form. She had landed on me with both boots planted squarely on my back, driving me to the roof floor face first, leaving me in a brutal push up position.

Peaches launched himself into her and drove her back a step. I rolled out from under one of her legs and turned my body to face her.

Without hesitation, she swung Stormchaser down in an attempt to cut me in half. I managed to just barely deflect the strike into the floor next to me and, using the floor as leverage, I kicked up into her face just as she punched down into my chest.

My foot connected with her jaw as her fist connected with my chest. All the air in my body decided it was the perfect moment to evacuate the premises. I heard the crack of the impact as my kick connected with her jaw. She stumbled back a few more steps while I wheezed for breath. Peaches jumped over me and straddled my body as I recovered. He took a deep breath and I covered my ears.

The runes on his flanks blazed with red energy, and I knew what was coming. There was no sonic protection on Ursula's roof.

He was going to unleash one of his obliterating barks.

This was going to hurt.

His bark was loud enough to make me wonder if a Harrier had decided to land right on top of us. A sonic boom crashed through the storm around us. The shockwave pushed us back, shoving Nan away from us across the wet floor.

When everything became silent, I lay in the middle of a devastated training area. I looked up into the night sky as the rain slowed, and then finally stopped.

I slowly turned my head to examine what was left of the training floor. It looked like we had unleashed a horde of angry rhinos on the roof.

Parts of the floor were missing; sections of the wall that enclosed the roof had holes in them. Some of the equipment that Ursula had used for training had been forcibly transformed into abstract art and mangled beyond recognition.

"Look at it this way," I said, slowly taking in the destruction. "You could always make this space a cutting-edge art gallery."

Nan laughed.

"Not funny, Strong," Ursula said. "I'm going to have to redo the entire training area."

"My apologies," Nan said.

When I looked across the floor, Nan was on one knee and smiling in my direction.

She looked slightly shredded.

She was bleeding from one side of her mouth, as well as from several cuts I didn't remember giving her; one of her eyes was partially swollen shut, too, and her combat armor had been torn in several places.

Peaches who had gone up against threats that had made me think twice, maybe even three times, had small bruises along his face and flanks. Aside from that, he looked fine.

I, on the other hand, looked as if I had wrestled with a group of angry ogres who had decided I needed to die tonight. My clothes were mangled. One leg of my jeans was torn, making me look very stylish. My jacket, which had been ripped off mid-fight, was missing a sleeve—not so stylish. My T-shirt had been torn in several sections, making me look like a mosh-pit escapee, if that mosh pit had been made up of trolls.

Judging from the heat I felt in my face, I could only imagine I looked as if I had stepped into a ring with Tyson for thirty rounds, and lost each one. My face and my body felt beaten to a pulp.

"You survived," Nan said, with a nod and getting to her feet. "Well done. You finally managed to execute a serviceable battle form." She turned to Ursula. "How long, Ursula?"

"Twenty seconds," Ursula said, looking down at a stop-watch. "From the moment of first transformation until he went down. This is the first successful attempt at the battle form."

"The first successful *unassisted* attempt," Nan corrected. "No divine help for this one."

"Twenty seconds?" I said, incredulous. "That's all? It felt like two hours."

"Aye," Nan said, shaking her head. "It's not much, but it's better than what you've done up to this moment. Twenty seconds in a heated conflict could save your life."

"Twenty seconds felt like nothing."

"In a real battle, it can make all the difference," she said. "It could buy you the precious time you or your allies need to survive."

"Let me guess: the only way to increase that time is to train like this?"

"Aye," she said, with a serious expression and a short nod. "In time, we will train you to the point that you will be able to enter and exit your battle form at will and with ease, without contact."

"Without contact?"

"Your battle form is a state of mind," she said, tapping her temple. "It doesn't, and shouldn't, require touch between you and your hellhound. You two are connected, bonded." She joined her two fists together, clasping her fingers. "You should be able to step into your battle form without touching him."

"For how long? Because that totally drained me," I said, with a groan. "My body feels like it weighs a ton. I could sleep for a month."

"In the beginning, two to three minutes—like today, but longer," she said. "Later on, two to three hours. If you ever get to the highest level of your battle form, a day or two at most, depending on your stamina. The weak link in the battle form is the human, not the hellhound."

"A day or two in that form?" I asked, surprised. "That sounds dangerous."

"It's usually fatal if held that long," she said, "for both you and your hellhound. It uses too many resources. But you have a special condition that should make it possible."

"It could kill him?" I asked, looking down at my hellhound. "We are never going that long."

"Not for a long time, no," she said. "We need to exploit your tolerances and slowly push you both to the outer limits of your abilities."

I stood in mild shock as she swung her axe in front of her body, repairing her combat armor and making it as good as new.

"I can't believe you could stand up to a hellhound in a battle form," I said. "Have you done this before, with a hellhound?"

"I've had practice."

"Practice?" I asked. "You make it a habit of fighting hellhounds?"

"Not hellhounds, no...a particular hellhound," she said, patting Peaches on his massive head and then patting the side of his body. "I'm sure you've met him. Hades has been generous enough to let me train with him."

"You've faced off against Cerberus?"

"I've *trained* against him," she said. "Facing off against a fully grown hellhound, one with the intent to kill, would most likely be fatal for anyone involved."

I just stared at her for close to five seconds.

FOUR

"You are insane."

"It has been remarked in the past."

"Are all of the Midnight Echelon that skilled?"

"No," she said, walking over to where I still lay. She extended an arm and lifted me to my feet effortlessly. "There's a reason why Dexter entrusted me with your training. There are many strong valkyrie who seek to join the numbers of the Midnight Echelon."

"Most of them don't make it?"

"Most do not," Nan said with a nod. "Out of all my valkyrie sisters, the Midnight Echelon is exceptional. We only number thirteen at last count."

"Thirteen? That's it?" I asked. "Out of all the valkyries?"

"Yes," she said. "Out of the thirteen, I am the tip of the spear. Maul and Braun are formidable. You haven't met many of the others. Only one other can match me in strength and ferocity; only one other can stand before me to the death, and perhaps survive."

"Let me guess, Vi?" I asked. "She can do it?"

"Yes," Nan said with a broad smile. "She is stronger than I

am, and slightly more insane—insane enough to attempt fighting me, and she has done so to a draw twice in the past. It is why she is the leader of the Midnight Echelon."

I moved slowly over to a bench and took a seat with a groan. My body ached as my curse worked overtime to heal me.

"Can we not do this again for a few years?"

Nan laughed and clapped me on the back, nearly dislocating a shoulder.

"This training was not only to improve your battle form," Nan said, gently gripping one of my shoulders with a vise-like grip. "The old man had questions regarding you and your blade."

"Ebonsoul?"

She nodded.

"There have been changes in you *and* your blade, having something to do with the First Elder Rune. He wanted me to test them," she said. "The best way to test these kinds of changes, is in the midst of a life-or-death battle."

"Were you really going to kill me?"

She narrowed her eyes at me, the smile gone.

"Did you doubt it?"

"Not for a second."

"Good," she said. "The goal for me was to test your immortality. Sadly, this time you survived. Perhaps next time."

"Next time? There's a next time?"

"Twenty seconds is unacceptable," she replied. "There will most certainly be a next time."

"A heads up on the extermination move would've been nice," I said, shaking my head. "What changes was Dex referring to?"

"Necrotic changes," she said, her voice dark. "You know your blade now has necrotic properties. Dexter wanted to see if they had manifested."

She raised a hand before I could ask.

"He will explain everything at the school, but I do have one question."

"Yes?"

"When you felt the energy form around your eyes, what did you think that was?

"The beginnings of a baleful glare?"

She gave me a long stare.

"Are you a hellhound?"

"As far as I know, no."

"Then what makes you think you can wield a baleful glare?"

"I mean, we're bondmates," I said, pursuing my logic. "I just assumed that if he can make a baleful glare, and I'm his bondmate—"

"That you should be able make a baleful glare?" she finished. "How hard and how often did I hit you?"

"Often, and I'm still recovering."

"You cannot make or wield a baleful glare," she said. "Your abilities are linked to the Mighty One, but they are not identical. Does that make sense?"

"You're asking me to make sense of things I barely have a grasp on," I said. "What *was* the energy around my eyes?"

"Dex will have answers for you," she said, avoiding the question. "Let's get you both ready. We leave in five minutes." She turned to Ursula. "My deepest thanks for the use of your space, Favored of Ukko. Do you need us to see to the repairs?"

"I have it taken care of," Ursula said. "Thank you."

"Are you sure?" I asked, looking around at the wrecked training area. "This is pretty bad."

"Strong, you do realize I'm responsible for the repairs of an entire metropolitan area, from Battery City to the center of Central Park, both, East and West? I don't think one rooftop is going to give me much trouble. I got this."

"I figured you would, but it doesn't hurt to ask," Nan said before swinging Stormchaser in a wide arc, forming a large portal. "We're off, then."

Nan motioned for Peaches and me to step forward.

"Thank you for the use of the space," I said. "I'd like to visit again when I get stronger."

"Whenever you feel ready, you're welcome to visit anytime," Ursula said. "Maybe one day we could even spar."

"I'm sure Peaches would love that."

"I'm sure he would," she said. "I'll see you all soon."

We stepped through the portal and Ursula's training space disappeared in a green haze.

FIVE

The green haze disappeared slowly, revealing a small hall.

The center of the hall was dominated by a large teleportation circle, which we stood in. The hall itself was made of rose marble, reminding me of the stone at the Wordweavers.

I had never seen this room at the school before—not that I had extensive knowledge of all the rooms in the Montague School of Battle Magic.

Standing near the circle and greeting us were Dex, Peanut, and Cece. I could tell the two girls were becoming fast friends. Part of me warmed at the knowledge that they were getting along. Another, more careful part of me was waving all the red flags surrounding the fact that these two young girls were becoming fast friends.

They both wore black jeans, and roamed around the school barefoot. That was where the similarities ended.

Cece wore a frosted blue T-shirt that read: *Let it go...or else.* The image on the shirt was of an ice mage unleashing an icy armageddon on an a group of approaching ogres.

I had the distinct feeling she had made the shirt herself.

Peanut, on the other hand, had gone for a full black

ensemble, the Morrigan's influence clearly visible in her stylistic choices. Her shirt read: *Some dwell in the light, others dwell in the shadows. I'm the one who makes them both feel fear.*

The image on her shirt was a pair of feral, red eyes over a canine mouth full of sharp, deadly teeth.

Both shirts were disturbing in their own way, and if I didn't personally know the two girls, I would be seriously concerned. Disturbing as their shirts may have been, both also raced over to Peaches and fawned over him with hugs and ample head and belly rubs.

I could see he was totally suffering as the girls fussed over him. Nan chuckled behind me as the girls began dragging my hellhound away with the promise of meat.

Being the diligent and responsible hellhound he was, he refused to be distracted and pulled away from his duties as my bondmate, choosing to stand by my side as the girls pulled on him.

That lasted all of three seconds as Dex made him a massive sausage which Cece and Peanut grabbed. They were about to walk away when they took a look at me.

"Wow," they said, in chorus. "What happened to you? You look shredded."

"Thanks," I said, looking down at what was left of my clothes, while Nan chuckled. I glanced in Nan's direction before answering. "I ran into a dangerous valkyrie and her axe."

"Bloody hell, boy," Dex said, giving me a once-over. "You let Nan bring you to such a state?"

"Bring me?" I asked. "I don't think I had much choice in the matter."

"Why don't you go with the sprites and get yourself a change of clothing," he said. "I have some matters to discuss with Nan before she leaves."

"She's leaving?" I asked, feigning disappointment. "That is sad news. I'm really going to miss our training sessions, Nan."

"Oh, I'm going," she said, "but I'll see you in a week or so. You're nowhere near where you need to be with your battle form."

"No need to rush on my account, really," I assured her, raising a hand in surrender. "Take a few weeks, even a month or two. I'm sure you have major Midnight Echelon business to deal with. You don't need—"

"You still don't understand, Strong," she said, stepping close to me and poking my chest with a finger with every word she said. "*You* are important Echelon business."

"I feel honored, really," I said, my voice and expression flat. "However will I contain all this privilege?"

"You should be," she said, moving away to stand next to Dex. "In fact, getting you into fighting shape is the most important Echelon business I have. You are an honorary member of the Midnight Echelon. Very few have stood with us on a battlefield and lived to tell the tale."

"Can I surrender my honorary status?"

"Of course," she said, turning back to glance at me. "The same way any other member of the Echelon does it."

I knew what was coming.

"You surrender your life in battle and you surrender your membership," she said, with a wicked smile. "See? Simple, really."

"So simple," I said as Cece tugged on my shirt. "I'll have to check my calendar and see if I'm open for another training session."

"Unless you're dead or in the process of becoming unalive due to an enemy trying to extinguish you—trust me, your calendar is open."

"Nan," Dex said, "walk with me." He turned to Peanut, who appeared to be both the stronger and more mature of the two young girls. "Girls, take him to get new clothes, then bring him back. Keep his hound busy." He stared at me. "Simon and I need to have some words."

"Why does that sound unpleasant?" I asked, as the girls pulled me out of the small hall. "Are we training today?"

"No more training today," he said, giving me another look. "Go get dressed in a respectable manner. We have standards here, you know."

He left me with my mouth open as he and Nan turned and walked away. Granted, he was dressed impeccably today, with a white dress shirt and black slacks. His hair was pulled back with a green sash, which kept his hair out of his eyes. Like the girls, he opted to go barefoot, and I couldn't blame him—it was the height of comfort. He had fully embraced the bohemian mage look.

"Does no one wear shoes in this school?" I asked. "What kind of uniform is this?" I motioned to their clothes. "T-shirt and jeans?"

"One of the best," Cece chimed in. "Sometimes we do have to wear formal uniforms, but they are amazing. They were designed by Aunt Mo."

I shook my head. I could only imagine a uniform designed by the Chooser of the Slain.

"Let me guess, black with black highlights?" I said. "Maybe a dash of green accents somewhere?"

"Wow," Peanut said. "Have you seen our uniforms? I don't think we've worn them while you were here. That's a great guess."

"I know the designer," I said. As they led me away and out of the hall. We made our way down a wide corridor which led into a large dining hall. "Where are we going? I've never seen this room. Is this the cafeteria?"

"One of them," Cece said. "We have a few. This one is for

the lower students. The upper classes have their own, and it's much bigger than this one."

I paused to look around.

Dex was really taking creating this School of Battle Magic seriously. On my last visit, I could see there were aspects that hadn't been finished.

This time, more of the property had been completed. Many of the rooms and campuses we passed had been furnished, and more buildings were visible on the school grounds.

"The school is really coming together," I said, turning in a circle as I took it all in. "Are you two happy here?"

They looked at each other first, before turning to face me.

"Yeah!" they both yelled. "This is the best school ever!"

"Sounds like you really like it here," I said, trying to calm them down. "Okay, how about you two take me somewhere I can get a change of clothes?"

"We can do that," Peanut said. "Follow us."

Before they headed off, they fed my voracious hellhound the sausage Dex had created for him. He inhaled the meat in record time and proceeded to slap the girls repeatedly with his tongue.

Both girls protested in the midst of giggles and pushed him away.

"Stop that!" they both called out as my hellhound generously droolified both of them. "Peaches! Stop!"

He stopped when they took off running, with Peaches easily matching their speed as they led us to one of the smaller, squat buildings on the other side of the dining hall.

SIX

We arrived at the smaller industrial-looking building, and the girls pointed inside.

"You can find clothes in there," Peanut said, pulling her hair back into a ponytail before pointing to a group of closets. "The clothes in there are brand new."

"Is this some kind of clothing warehouse?" I asked, looking inside the building. "What is this place?"

"Something like that," Cece said. "If you want a new set of clothing, look in the closets. Unless you really like what you're wearing"—she turned up her nose at my shredded wardrobe with the practiced expression that I'd swear she learned from Monty—"then go to the mirror in the last room on the ground floor and stand in front of it. It's the room with the brass door. There's a sign on the door that says Mirror Room."

"Mirror Room?" I asked. "What does the mirror do? Am I going to end up in another dimension or something? Is this some kind of prank?"

"That's not this mirror, Mr. Simon," Cece said. "We wouldn't send you to *that* mirror." She looked at me as if I was as bright as a bag of bricks. "If we did, then we wouldn't be able to find you. Uncle Dex would get mad if we sent you to that mirror." She glanced at Peanut. "He didn't like the last time we used it."

They both broke out in a secretive laugh that was full of mischief. Whatever that mirror was, they had tried it and had gotten in trouble.

"What happened the last time you used that mirror?" I asked. "You know, the mirror you were expressly told not to use?"

Normally, I would've left it alone—you know, kids being kids and curious. I can't even remember all the trouble I got into, doing things I wasn't supposed to do, but this was different. I was dealing with two young girls who could easily team up and form a new threat to the plane, named Mayhem and Destruction, with both titles being interchangeable.

It was best not to take any chances.

"Nothing that bad...really," Peanut said. "We just had some unwanted visitors, and Uncle Dex got real red in the face when he saw what we did. Honestly, I think he and Aunt Mo were secretly impressed, but didn't dare say so, because that would be *encouraging us*."

She said the last two words with air quotes.

They both broke out in more giggles and side glances. These two were going to be serious trouble in a few years. They were probably serious trouble right now. They would be cataclysmic trouble in a few years. I really hoped Dex knew what he was doing by keeping them together *and* training them.

I did my best to keep a straight face and poured extra sternness into my voice when I answered them, in an effort to give them a sense of seriousness about their situation.

"You two need to follow the rules Dex and the Morrigan set, especially rules about the artifacts in this school. It's for your own good and safety," I said, keeping my voice low and somber. "You don't want to get in trouble with either of them. Trust me, it's not worth it."

They were about to turn and leave the warehouse, but Peanut stopped and looked at me. As young as she was, she had the gaze of an ancient. She paused, nodded, fixing me with a piercing look, a look that exposed too much pain for someone so young, and stared into the depths of my soul—or at least it felt that way.

"Do *you* always follow the rules, Mr. Simon?" Peanut asked. "Always? You've never broken them? You've never broken *one* rule...ever?"

"Yeah, do we?" Cece asked with a small smile, probably remembering when I encouraged her to break through my dawnward, despite the instructions we were given. "Or do you sometimes bend the rules yourself?"

I had a choice here.

I could give them the standard adult answer, but by this point, their BS detector was calibrated to Frontier supercomputer levels. They would see right through any half-truth I could give them, no matter how finely devised—especially since they lived with Dex and the Morrigan, two masters of speaking and deciphering riddles.

On the other hand, I couldn't advise them to break all the rules, because I knew Dex would chew my ear off for encouraging them to disregard any kind of order.

I had to strike a delicate balance, and running away from the conversation was not an option.

My hellhound sat back on his haunches, clearly interested in the conversation, staring up at me as if to say: *I, too, would be curious to hear your thoughts on this topic, bondmate.*

"Okay, girls," I said, after taking a deep breath. "Here is my advice on following rules while you live here at the Montague School of Battle Magic."

They both nodded, paying attention.

"What is the name of the school?" I continued. "The full name?"

"The Montague School of Battle Magic for Gifted Mages," Peanut said proudly. "*That* is the full name."

"It is?" I said, surprised at the extended name. "Really?"

"Yes, really," Cece said. "You didn't know?"

"Well, I had an idea. I was just making sure you two knew the correct name," I said, trying to recover and failing. "It would look bad if you didn't even know the name of your own school, don't you think?"

"Suuure," Cece said, giving Peanut a knowing glance. "You were making sure *we* knew the full name. Right."

Honestly, I had no idea the school would be teaching gifted mages. It made sense, though. Monty was some sort of prodigy, and these two were clearly ahead of the curve for their age—not that I had any context for gauging the skill of mages.

I had it on good authority that Peanut wasn't even a mage, but I knew she was scary powerful, whatever she was. Dex was off-the-charts on the power scale, and I didn't even try to quantify the Morrigan.

How do you rate a goddess like her? Do you use a scale from scary to petrifying to heart-stopping fear?

I shook my thoughts free and returned to the topic.

"Fine, full disclosure, I didn't know the full name," I said. "Dex must have added the 'gifted mages' part when I was away."

"We'll give you a pass for being honest," Peanut said. "We wouldn't want you to look bad for not knowing the name of what is going to be the best and most dangerous school of gifted battle mages ever. Go ahead, we're listening."

I had no doubt regarding the future reputation of this

school. It was certainly on track for being the most dangerous with these two alone.

"Okay," I continued, focusing on the girls. "The name on the school is Montague. So, who sets the rules?"

"The Morrigan!" they both called out simultaneously. "Well, it says Uncle Dex's last name, but she sets most of the rules."

"She does?" I asked, confused. "He doesn't set any of them?"

"He tried," Cece said with a laugh. "Then she went and changed it, and he said, 'Aye, that makes more sense. We'll keep it that way.'"

"She does that *all* the time," Peanut added. "Though sometimes when he's really mad, he'll make up a rule because one of us did something we weren't supposed to do."

"What happens then?" I asked, genuinely curious. "Does he keep the rule?"

"For a few days," Peanut answered. "Then Aunt Mo will whisper something in his ear and he'll get his goofy smile, and there goes that rule."

"Okay, I think I need to adjust my answer to your question."

"Really?" Cece asked. "So, do you always follow the rules?"

"I think the answer that you're going to learn in the walls of this particular school is—it depends," I said. "There have been times when I have followed the rules. Especially when Monty or Peaches were in trouble, and if I hadn't followed the rules, they would have gotten hurt, badly."

They both nodded, understanding.

"There are other times though, when following the rules would've made things worse," I said. "In those cases, I could have lost my friends or family by following the rules."

"That's when you made them feel pain, right?" Peanut asked almost too eagerly, which worried me a bit. "You let them know what happens to those who try to hurt those close to you and make them regret it, right?"

"Well, we always try diplomacy first—"

"Diplomacy," Cece asked pensively. "Is that when you shoot first and ask questions later?"

"No, that's—" I started.

"No," Peanut added. "Diplomacy is when you use overwhelming power to show your enemies they have no chance and should give up right away or suffer a painful death. Right?"

"What? No!" I said, raising my voice. "Diplomacy is when you try to resolve problems using just your words, not violence."

They both burst out laughing.

I waited while they composed themselves again.

"Wait, you're serious?" Peanut asked. "You can actually do that?"

"Yes, it is possible."

"How often has *that* worked?" Cece asked, her voice serious. "Have you and Mr. Tristan solved problems just using your words?"

"Well…We've tried," I said, trying to stay at least in the neighborhood of honest responses. "It hasn't always worked."

"Meaning it's *never* worked," Peanut said, shaking her head as her expression grew hard. "Some people—bad people—won't listen to words. Some people only understand pain. They only stop when they know you're stronger than they are and can hurt them."

"Not always, but yes, that is true," I said, not wanting to sugarcoat anything. "Some people only understand violence. Those are the ones who will try to use rules to hurt or control you."

"Like when those bad people said I broke the rules and

they needed to take my powers away," Peanut said, looking away. "That was not a good time to follow the rules."

"No, no it wasn't," I said. "Same goes for you, Cece. One of the reasons you're at this school is because you're so strong. The rules say you shouldn't use your ability."

"But how will I get stronger if I can't use my ability?" Cece asked. "I need to practice."

"Exactly," I said. "In order to get stronger, you have to practice. You have to use your ability, but you can't do that back at home—not without damaging the building and getting your Aunt Olga upset."

"So I have to break that rule?"

"Within reason," I said, raising a hand. "Dex and the Morrigan have created a space for the both of you, and others like you, to practice, train, and increase in power."

"But we can't break the school," Peanut said. "Uncle Dex is always yelling at us not to break the school."

"Why do you think that is?"

"Because he likes the buildings in one piece?" Peanut answered. "He's tired of fixing the broken walls and floors?"

I smiled at the thought of Dex having to constantly repair the damage being caused by these two girls.

"I'm sure that has something to do with it, but it's more," I said. "Something I'm still learning."

I thought to my recent training session of destruction at Ursula's.

"Something you're still learning?" Cece asked. "What are *you* still learning?"

"Just because you have the power to destroy something, doesn't mean you should."

"But what if you can't control your power?" Cece asked. "What if it gets away from you?"

"Then you practice until you can," I said as the realization dawned on me. "How can you help your friends or your family if you can't control your power?"

"You can't," Peanut answered. "The only way is to have enough power to protect those you care about."

"Yes, and there's more," I said. "One day, you won't be just students at this school."

"We won't?"

"One day, I'm certain both of you will be teachers or staff of some kind, helping run the school," I said. "In a place like this, you have to lead by example. Why would the students listen to you two if you're going around destroying the place?"

"That's a good point," Cece said. "You're really smart, Mr. Simon."

"Just Simon," I said. "I've have some experience, but I wasn't born into this world like you two. By the time you get to my age, you two will be amazing. Listen to Dex and the Morrigan, follow the rules as best as you can, always look out for each other, and you will both be beyond amazing."

"Really?" they both asked with hope in their eyes. "You think so?"

"I know so," I said. "Now, point me to this mirror. I need to get my new clothes."

"There's no need," another voice said behind us. "Girls, I'm sure there are chores that need attending to, yes?"

"Yes, Aunt Mo," they both said. "Can we take Peaches with us?"

"Yes," the Morrigan said, materializing behind me and nearly giving me a heart attack, "as long as Simon agrees."

I nodded and the girls giggled as they took off with my hellhound in tow. I could tell that he was really torn about leaving with the girls, as evidenced by his half-a-second moment of hesitation before he bounded off with them.

"Make sure he doesn't chew on anything!" the Morrigan

called out as the girls disappeared around a corner. "Did you hear me?"

"Yes, Aunt Mo," came the distant reply. "We'll watch him! No chewing on anything!"

The Morrigan turned to face me and smiled.

My blood turned to ice, and I looked around for the nearest exit.

"Come with me, Simon," she said, part promise and part threat. "I will fix you."

I followed her down the corridor.

SEVEN

"Really, I'm fine," I said. "No fixing needed. I just need to repair my clothing and I'm good to go."

"Come," she said, giving me no option. "I'll take care of you."

"It would be really great if you were a bit more specific," I said, as I followed her. "When you say things like, 'I'll fix you,' or, 'I'll take care of you,' it sounds kind of fatal. Know what I mean?"

"No," she said, as we kept walking. "What else would I mean? Your clothes are in tatters and you need them repaired. What else could I mean besides fixing your clothing?"

I was about to respond when I realized that would only get me in a deeper situation that would be even harder to escape, so I opted for remaining silent as we walked.

We walked down a narrow corridor which led to a plain-looking door. Beyond the door, we stepped into a large, cozy office filled with books of all kinds.

For a moment, I thought we had taken a detour into the library, and not the Morrigan's office.

The large plaque on the desk read: *The Morrigan—Dean of Student Affairs*. I looked around quickly and realized that this office felt lived in and comfortable.

"This place feels—I don't know—warm?" I said, looking around and taking in the office. "Nice. It's welcoming. The fireplace is a nice touch. Makes it feel homey."

"Don't sound so surprised, Simon," she said, sitting behind her large desk. "Did you expect my office to be dark and painfully frigid, located in the depths of the lowest dungeon with vermin covering the floors, and spiders adorning the corners?"

"I want to say...no?" I said, hedging my bets. "I honestly didn't know what to expect from your office. This is cozier than the last time I was here."

She smiled and then nodded, motioning to one of the large wingback chairs in front of her desk.

"Please, sit."

I sat and sunk into the comfortable chair. She steepled her fingers, leaning back in her chair, and gazed at me. My level of awkwardness went from "mild" to "escape this room —now" in the span of five seconds.

It wasn't just that the Morrigan embodied a primal fear. She took that fear and in the context of a school—even this school—she added all my educational horror stories to the mix.

Every trip to the principal's office, every time I was threatened with having my parents called—which were enough times that several Deans and Principals had my home number on speed dial—and the countless detentions where I was the guest of honor for one infraction or another...they all came back full force under her calm and self-assured gaze of quiet destruction.

"I heard what you told the girls," she said, still staring at me with those eyes that peered into my soul. No student at this school was going to be able to escape that gaze for more than a second or two. I almost pitied them. "Why did you answer them that way?"

I cleared my throat as I thought back to my response.

"I tried to give them an answer that would help them, not just today, but always," I said. "I can understand their position rationally, but I can't empathize. They're just kids. Most of the time, I'm out of my depth in this world. How are they supposed to navigate the world they're in?"

"With difficulty."

"Everything about this world is difficult...for adults," I countered. "It's impossible for two kids their age."

"How do you think the adults arrive in this world? Fully grown?"

"I just meant to navigate the complicated parts," I corrected. "It's hard enough for adults. It must be nearly impossible for children."

"They are both more mature than you can imagine."

"I have no doubt, but they can make mistakes," I said. "Make a mistake in the normal world and you get yelled at, maybe grounded. If you make a mistake in this world, you end up with a building in a deep-freeze, or unleashing orbs of super destruction that wipe out everything."

"The stakes are certainly higher," she said. "There is that."

"So it seems impossible for them at this age."

"Yes and no," she said. "Imagine knowing what you know now, but at their age?"

"I would be freaking out of my mind," I said, shaking my head. "I'm *still* freaking out about everything I can and can't do."

"You are 'freaking out' because you didn't have a place to study, a place to call home—like this school," she answered, looking around the office. "Tristan doesn't suffer from frequent 'freak outs', does he?"

"Monty? You're kidding," I said, staring at her in disbelief. "I've seen him face an ogre trying to pound us to dust. While death is on the way, he'll stop to create a shield, along with some finger wiggles to stop the angry ogre, and while *that's* going on, he's lecturing me on the deeper workings of quantum magic."

"He is a mage, after all."

"Then he'll explain how 'everything is connected' if I just allowed myself to feel the underlying interlocking networks of energy lattices. Monty does not freak out...ever."

"That does sound like Tristan," she said. "Do you know why he is that way?"

"Not enough playtime as a child?" I said. "Early exposure to energy manipulation drains the fun out of children and makes them overly serious and analytical?"

"Neither," she said. "Tristan was a happy boy, and one full of mischief."

"I'm sorry, for a moment there, I thought you said Monty had been a happy child full of mischief," I said, waggling a finger in one of my ears. "I must have heard wrong."

"You didn't. Even though he was raised in what was considered ideal circumstances, something was lacking."

"He was never given a sense of humor?"

She sighed and I realized I was really pushing my luck.

"I understand. This topic being so close to home, may make it difficult for you to face," she said. "But face it you must. Why is Tristan the way he is?"

"He grew up in a sect," I said. "They trained him to be that way."

"Only partially correct. Despite his training, there is something lacking," she said. "Wouldn't you agree?"

"I agree he could lighten up just a bit," I said. "It really wouldn't hurt his face to smile. I won't say more because that would imply he smiles occasionally."

"If you contrast the two Montagues, you know what the differences are?" she asked. "On the surface, what do you see?"

"Monty takes everything too seriously, including himself, which makes him seem grumpy most of the time, and angry all of the time."

"And Dexter?"

"Dex comes across as if nothing is too serious, but that's not entirely true," I said, giving it some thought. "I've seen Dex angry and serious. I'd have to say the biggest difference besides the enormous gap in power is their temperaments. Dex laughs often; Monty laughs...never. At this point, I don't know if he even *can* laugh. He might pull something if he tried."

"Your conclusion, then?"

"Monty, even though he was raised in a sect—the best environment for a mage—is still missing how to live life," I said, "and Dex, who I can only guess was raised by wild wolves, knows how to embrace life and enjoy every moment."

"A fair and accurate assessment, except for the wild wolves part," she said with a smile. "Dex never grew up in a sect. He grew up in a setting closer to this one—a school: the first Golden Circle, before it became an official sect."

"I thought a sect was the best place for a mage to study and grow?" I said. "Isn't that what sects are designed to be? Schools for mages?"

"And yet Tristan recently took several steps down a dark path by pursuing blood runes and the First Elder Rune," she said. "Even a sect like the Golden Circle, a place designed for this kind of learning, left him ill-prepared for the challenges he now faces."

"Is he going dark...again?" I asked, concerned about the sudden shift in topic. "Keeper Evergreen removed—"

"No, he is not going dark," she said, looking across to her

books. "We will discuss your bond-brother in a moment, but first I would like you to please elaborate further on your response to the girls. Why should they follow rules?"

"I didn't want to tell them to disregard all rules," I said, "despite the fact that Dex isn't exactly a shining example of what a mage who follows the rules does."

She laughed.

"You do have a point there," she said, "Dex does have an aversion to certain rules. Especially those governing dress. Speaking of"—she narrowed her eyes at me—"is this some sort of avant-garde fashion statement you're making with this attire?"

I looked down at my shredded clothes.

"No statement," I said. "I was just on my way to a wardrobe mirror the girls were sharing with me to get a new set of clothes."

"No need," she said with a wave of her hand. My clothes were instantly restored. "There, good as new. Better than new."

"Better than new?"

"Your clothing has been re-runed," she said. "How did you let one of the Midnight Echelon bring you to such a state? Were you with your hellhound?"

"Yes," I said. "It was battle form training."

"You were in a battle form *with* your hellhound?"

"Well, yes," I said. "I'm still trying to get the hang of it."

"How long did you hold the form?"

"Twenty seconds—but I think it was longer—and I'm still on the lowest level of the battle form."

"Clearly," she said with a raised eyebrow. "Still, twenty seconds should have been enough for you to fight a member of the Midnight Echelon to a stalemate. The state of your clothing makes it appear as if you were there for target practice."

"It felt like that too," I said. "Just to be clear, we *are* speaking about the same Midnight Echelon?"

"Who did you face?"

"Nan and that oh-so-friendly axe of hers."

"Hanna did this to you?"

"I've never called her that, but yes, she pounded me pretty well."

"And she battered you by herself?" she asked, narrowing her eyes at me. "Were you fighting her with your eyes closed, or an arm tied behind your back? Tell me you had some type of handicap."

"The only handicap I had was not being able to master my battle form with Peaches for longer."

"That is not a handicap," she scoffed. "Have you forgotten whom you have faced? One valkyrie, even if she is of the Midnight Echelon, should not pose such difficulty to the Marked of Kali and bondmate to the scion of Cerberus. Have you forgotten who you are, *Aspis*? Have you forgotten that you wield a necrotic seraph, a blade capable of rending the veil between this world and the next?"

"Excuse me? What?" I asked, surprised. "Can you back up a bit there? A blade capable of rending what?"

"We will get to that later," she said, waving my questions away. "Let's get back to your answer. You were saying?"

EIGHT

There was no use in trying to press her to answer me. What was I going to do—force the Morrigan to answer my question or else?

Or else what?

Going down that route only made sense if I wanted to get crushed into Simon paste after I pissed her off.

I would have to be patient.

"I gave them that answer because it was the right one to give them," I said, after some thought. "They may not know what this world holds for them, but I'm certain there's a fair amount of danger involved. I don't know what this world holds for me, but I do know that strictly following the rules is a good way to get squashed."

"Colorful, but apt."

"You and Dex are training them," I continued. "I seriously doubt you want them to be mindless robots. You're going to teach them to be critical thinkers, to listen with their brains and their guts. Sometimes, that means bending the rules, and sometimes, that means breaking them."

"You have done both," she said. "Why didn't you share some of your exploits?"

"That would be a bad idea, and probably boring to them," I said, shaking my head. "Except for the part where things get blown up or destroyed. The last thing I need is Dex giving me a dressing down because I corrupted his students with bad examples of what not to do."

"Corrupted?" she asked innocently, but I knew I had ventured into dangerous territory. If this conversation had been a forest, I had just crossed the sign warning me of man-eating wolves in the area, ready to rip my arms off and beat me silly with them, as I bled out. "What do you mean by... corrupted? Do you think the girls are *corrupted*?"

"Absolutely not," I said quickly. "Nor do I think they are corruptible."

"Oh, they *are* corruptible. We all are," she said with a small smile that chilled me to my core. "Especially wielding so much power and being so young. How would you handle that situation? A child with that level of destruction within?"

"Before I continue, can I ask you a question?"

She smiled again and I nearly reconsidered.

"Of course," she said, her voice still light, but her eyes warning me of an impending maiming. "You and I have an *understanding*, don't we?"

Never in my life had I ever wanted to redefine a word more. I was beginning to grasp that the words I thought I knew didn't always mean what I thought they meant.

"You and I do," I said, treading carefully. "Badb Catha and I may have a different kind of *understanding*."

"No, we are all one," she said, her voice a blade slicing through the office—which was, all of a sudden, not so cozy, as the temperature hovered near arctic for a few seconds. "Ask your question."

"You just said we are all corruptible," I continued,

measuring my words around the cracking as I stepped out onto the thin ice that was the conversation I found myself in. "Does that include you, too?"

She remained silent for a few seconds as she stared at me.

"All throughout recorded history and before human history, gods have existed," she said. "You only need to study the pantheons to understand that gods, like humans, can be petty, cruel, vindictive...and, yes, corrupt. I have been guilty of some of those qualities, but I am not, and have never been, corrupt. My role and composition in the larger scheme of things serves as a check and balance against my succumbing to corruption."

"So you *can't* become corrupt?"

"What does absolute power do, Simon?"

"Corrupt absolutely," I said. "But you don't have absolute power."

"But I'm close," she said as green energy raced across her eyes. "And I am not corrupt not because the possibility doesn't exist, but rather because I value my role greater than anything any corruption can ever offer."

"Is it harder for you because you are triune?"

She smiled again, and this time I knew I had crossed a line.

"Are you asking because you would like to continue having this conversation with Badb Catha? Or do you wish to converse with Macha? Either one would prove...illuminating."

There was another word I was certain I knew the meaning to, but when she used it, sounded like it meant *excruciating*.

"You know what? I'm perfectly content just speaking with you."

"A wise choice," she said. "Now...answer my question. How would you handle a child with the power of untold destruction within?"

She leaned back and bore through me with her pitch-black eyes which shimmered with green energy every few seconds. I gave her question thought. There was no way I was going to escape answering her. When the Morrigan asked you a question, she expected an answer.

"That's not just those two girls," I said, raising a hand as she raised an eyebrow. "Hear me out. Yes, those two have access to more power than most kids their age. They have access to more power than a few mages I've run across. But it's not just them. That potential for destruction is in everyone."

"So they are doomed?" she asked. "Shall I erase them from existence?"

"No," I said, shaking my head. "That's a little extreme, don't you think?"

"It all depends on your perspective," she said matter-of-factly. "If they are a future evil, wouldn't it make more sense to excise them now to save others later?"

"You don't know if they're a future evil," I countered, getting upset. "You can't go around excising people like a cancer based on a potential evil. If that were the case, do you know how many people would bite the dust?"

Then I realized I was speaking to the Chooser of the Slain. She actually probably did know how many would bite the dust if that was the policy. For all I knew, it had been the policy many times in the past.

She must have seen me come to that exact realization because she smiled at me again, causing my stomach to twist into a painful knot.

I took a deep breath, calmed down and re-centered. It had occurred to me that not all life-and-death struggles happened with deadly weapons on a designated battlefield.

Some battles occurred in a cozy office while sitting in a

wingback chair, discussing the fates of future mages with the Chooser of the Slain.

I gathered my thoughts and discovered my voice again.

I cleared my throat a few times before speaking.

"The key is how you nurture them, how they're taught and trained. Too much discipline and you create a tyrant; too much slack, in the other extreme, and you create something just as bad—someone easily swayed by desire. The key is to strike a balance between the two."

She nodded and tapped her chin as she thought on my answer.

"Discipline tempered by healthy nurturing," she said. "Giving the student room to grow with strong parameters. I like it. You are going to make an excellent instructor at this school."

"An excellent what?" I asked, surprised. "I don't teach. I barely learn. Haven't you been keeping up with my life recently? I am not instructor material. What would I teach? How to destroy things? And I especially don't teach kids. This is a school for gifted mages. I'm pretty sure there are certain qualifications involved in teaching people with that title."

"You seem to be under the impression that I was *asking* you," she said. "The time will come when you *will* be an instructor at this school. It's not a matter of if, but *when*. You and Tristan both will be part of the faculty at this school."

"Don't you care about these kids?"

"Are you insinuating I'm placing the children in harm's way by exposing them to you and your instruction?"

"No, no," I said, raising my hands in surrender. "It's just that—"

"It's settled, then," she finished, and now I realized how she passed rules in the school. This was a battle I had lost before I even knew I was involved in a battle at all. She could have taught Sun Tzu a few things about the art of warfare. "I will give you the time needed to create the curriculum for your class. You still have plenty of time. Plenty of time."

"Of course I do," I said. "Will there be anything else?"

She looked off to the side and nodded.

"Dex is looking for you," she said as she grabbed a stack of papers. "He will be in the rare-book library with Tristan. Thank you for a most productive conversation. I do so enjoy our talks."

"You're welcome...I think?"

She smiled again.

"I think I'm going to enjoy our frequent conversations."

"I better go see what Dex wants," I answered, getting to my feet and heading for the door. "Thank you again."

"No, Simon," she said, waving a hand and causing the door to open for me. "Thank you."

I practically ran out of her office.

NINE

I skidded down the corridor and made a sharp turn at the corner. I followed the signs and found myself at the rare-book library ten minutes later.

It wasn't because the library was so close to her office, but more because I couldn't move fast enough to put distance between the Morrigan and me.

"Slow down, boy," Dex said when I slid into the rare-book library. "Who's chasing you?"

He looked past me into the corridor and then focused on me.

"Chasing me? Why would anyone be chasing me? No one's chasing me—I just wanted to get the blood flowing. Exercise is good for the body."

Dex narrowed his eyes at me for a few seconds and then chuckled.

"Ach, you been speaking to Mo, haven't ye?"

"Why would you say that?" I said, nervously. "I was just wandering the school grounds. You've made some amazing renovations. Really impressive."

He laughed again.

"No need to deny it," he said, as Monty wandered into the library. "She unnerves most people—ask the lad here. Nephew, how have your training sessions with the Morrigan been?"

Monty had slowly entered the library, holding a cup of Earl Grey. He was dressed in a typical Zegna suit jacket, a pale-blue dress shirt, no tie, casual pants, and a pair of Armani loafers.

He was practically slumming.

"Unsettling," Monty said, before taking a long pull from his cup. "I thought facing TK at the Reckoning was challenging. I'd rather go through that again than do more of these tutoring sessions with the Morrigan."

"That bad?" I asked. "It can't be *that* bad."

"How long did you just spend with her—in her office, I'm assuming?"

"I don't know," I said, thinking back to my recent encounter with Bone-chilling Fear disguised as Dex's love interest. "I want to say about ten to fifteen minutes, but it felt like three hours."

"Sounds about right," Monty said, and looked off into the distance for close to twenty seconds. "Felt like three hours."

"Monty?" I said and glanced at Dex. "You okay?"

For a moment, I thought he had suffered a mental break of some kind. Dex held up a hand and motioned for me to be patient.

"Sorry, I'm still processing," he said, snapping back to himself. "Did you know the Morrigan doesn't need to sleep?"

"Don't I know it," Dex said, with a wide grin. "The woman is indefatigable in every sense of the word."

"Thank you for that," I protested, with a groan. "How many senses of that word exist?"

"Quite a few, actually. Would you like me to describe them to you?" Dex asked. "When she gets going—"

"No, thank you...really," I said. "I have enough to scar my imagination for a month at least, thanks."

"I just spent the last six hours going over basic casts with her," Monty said with a haunted voice. "She wanted to make sure I had an *understanding* of the foundational casts before moving on to the intermediate material."

"An understanding?" I asked, with a shudder. "That can't be good."

"It was...unpleasant."

"And intermediate?" I continued, surprised. "Not even the advanced? You were close to Archmage last time I recall. What happened?"

"I should consider myself fortunate she is even willing to look at intermediate casts so soon after Evergreen removed the First Elder Rune along with the other blood runes, or so I'm told."

"Why?"

"Because if he was heavy-handed with Tristan, he could have done serious damage," Dex said. "Damage we wouldn't see until it's too late, if we move right back to advanced casts."

"What are you saying? Monty has to go back to being a basic mage?" I asked, confused. "I thought he was a few shifts away from Archmage? Now, all of a sudden he's back to being an apprentice?"

"There's nothing wrong with mastering or reviewing the basics," Dex said, with an edge to his voice that led me to believe there was more going on than he was letting on. "I still practice the basics...every day."

"But Monty isn't a basic mage," I said. "He wasn't a basic mage when we met, and he's certainly not a basic mage now. What's going on?"

"That was my initial argument when I met with her six hours ago," Monty said, shaking his head. "She refused to circumvent the process. It was going to take six hours, and it took six hours."

"Did you say six hours? Consecutively?"

"I tried to break it up over three days, but surprisingly my suggestion was declined. Imagine that."

"Six hours," I said, my voice barely above a whisper. "How are you still coherent? How is your brain still working?"

"She demonstrated mercy at this level," he said, before taking another long pull of his tea. "The next level promises to be longer and more unrelenting. She wants to know if Evergreen altered something he shouldn't have."

"That wasn't her," Dex said. "That was me. I asked her to check you."

"Thank you for that, Uncle," Monty said, his voice laced with anger. "Any other tortures you're saving for later? Perhaps you could spring a surprise lobotomy on me? It would certainly be less painful."

"Stop your whining, and you're welcome," Dex snapped. "Someone had to check you."

"Check me?" Monty asked. "I could always go to Haven—"

"No, not for this kind of diagnosis," Dex said. "Roxanne wouldn't even know what to look for; or, what not to look for. She can't operate at a Keeper's level. It's too elevated for her. His casts are too nuanced, too layered. If he left something—"

"Left something?" Monty asked. "What could he have possibly left behind? Are you certain you're not just being paranoid?"

"It's only paranoia when no one is after you, nephew," Dex said. "There were, and still are, several groups after you. Do I need to remind you of this?"

"No," I said, realizing he was right. "Dira is still in the wind."

I knew Dira was still out there somewhere, and I had no illusion she had just forgotten about me and gone on an extended vacation to Antarctica. I could hope, but I knew she was only biding her time, and knowing her, she was leveling up and getting better weapons before we crossed paths again.

"Not just her," Dex said. "Verity hasn't folded up shop; they would like to see the both of you cease breathing. Then. You have the Blood Hunters." He pointed at me. "There seems to be a particularly violent splinter of that group that has a special hate for you and your vampire. Any reason why?"

"Because I didn't let a member of their faction barbecue Michiko," I said. "She took it personally—probably because I took one of her arms."

"Aye, that has a way of staying with a person," Dex said, with a nod. "Well, there are rumblings that they're looking for you, too."

"Not surprising. Chi told me as much the last time we spoke," I said. "She said, she was moving on that information. I don't know what that means, but we're going to try and settle this without bloodshed, at least at first."

"Good luck with that," Dex answered. "There's more, besides your diagnosis."

"More?" Monty asked. "So it's not just a review of rudimentary casts?"

"No, lad," Dex answered, and glanced at me. "There've been some...developments."

"Why does that always sound negative?" I asked. "It's never, 'There've been some developments. You've just earned yourself a three-month vacation on a beach in Fiji!' Or even better, 'We've developed a way you can have a lifetime supply of Death Wish just by thinking about it'. Now *that* would be a development. No, it's always something you want to avoid."

Dex turned to me as he stood and began walking out of the library. He motioned for us to follow him.

"Walk with me."

"Uncle Dex?" Monty asked, and I heard the concern in his voice. "Is everything all right? With you, I mean?"

"Are you daft, child?" Dex snapped, as he glanced at Monty. "I'm telling you that your lives are in danger, and you're worried about me and my health? How hard did Mo hit you this morning?"

"Apparently not hard enough," Monty said. "Apologies."

"None needed," Dex said, his voice somewhat softer. "I'm the one who should be apologizing. I should have told you about the diagnosis I asked Mo to do, but I didn't want to concern you needlessly."

"She found something, didn't she?" Monty said. "Evergreen left something?"

"I don't know," Dex said. "All I have are pieces of a big puzzle, and the picture they make doesn't look good."

Something was bothering him, but the process couldn't be rushed. If there was one thing I learned about dealing with my elders, it was that they were usually set in their ways, with little room for improvisation. He would share it his way when he was ready, and not before then.

We just had to buckle up for the ride.

"Do you know what she found?" I asked. "Can you tell us that much?"

"Tell me about your training with Nan," Dex told me, approaching me out of left field. "How did that go?"

"I don't see what my training has to do—?"

"Humor an old man," he said, cutting me off. "Tell me about your training with Nan."

"It went about as good as I expected," I answered. "She bounced me all over Ursula's training floor. And, if I'm being honest, I think she was holding back. There were a few times she could have ended me and she didn't."

"Give me the pertinent details," Dex said, clipping his words short while looking down. The three of us had left the interior of the library and were outside the building, heading over to one of the large gardens just across from the main dining hall. "Situational information."

"Situational information? Got it," I said, with a curt nod. "It was a dark and stormy night."

"Boy...your smart ass is going to bring you pain in the very near future," Dex threatened. "What the bloody hell does that mean?"

"I'm just giving you the facts," I said. "Nan wanted us to train outside, and then she asked Ursula to go all thunder god with her discount Mjolnir, and it started raining."

"Just rain? I'm surprised."

"It was just rain for the first few minutes, and then we entered a full-blown monsoon season," I clarified. "I could barely stand with the wind and the rain on a wet roof, and then Nan wants to start swinging that menace of a weapon around."

Dex gave me a huge grin.

"That sounds more like it," he said with a nod. "Don't let the Bear hear you call her hammer a discount Mjolnir. She's a tad touchy about the subject."

"She should have asked for Mjolnir instead of settling for a knock-off."

"Boy, I'm serious," Dex said. "Not only are you risking the Bear, but you are risking offending Ukko—the original owner of said hammer—who also happens to be a god of thunder, lightning, and strength. Which one of those qualities would you like to be on the angry end of?"

"None," I said, quickly. "Once the hurricane got started, Nan decided to start the party for real."

"What do you mean, for real?"

"There were a few moments when it felt like she really was going to cut me with Stormchaser," I said. "She also has a mean right cross. She nearly dislocated my jaw several times."

Dex chuckled.

"Aye, that she does," he said. "She was pushing your limits, taking you to the edge where you didn't have time to think, only react."

"I was there," I said. "I could barely stand still. She had me moving, dodging, striking, evading, and reacting. Forget time to think, I barely had time to breathe."

"Tell me about the eyes," Dex said—I guessed he had been briefed by Nan. "What happened to your eyes?"

"Your eyes?" Monty asked, alarm in his voice. "Yes, what happened to your eyes?"

"Energy and power started flowing into them," I said, slightly taken aback at Monty's reaction. "That is, until Nan shut it down. Then, it was mostly pain."

"I think you'd better go into some more detail about the eyes," Dex said. "It's pertinent to the developments."

TEN

"There's not much to tell," I said as we entered the large garden. I noticed Monty was being more silent than his usual grumpy self. "One moment, I was feeling all kinds of power from the battle form."

"This power," Dex said. "What did it feel like, exactly?"

"It felt like my eyes were burning, but from the inside," I said. "I thought I was going to unleash a baleful glare."

"Why?" Dex asked. "Are you a hellhound?"

"No," I said, raising a hand. "I went through this with The Morrigan, and she already made me feel silly for suggesting it."

"No judgment," Dex said, serious. "No one here is a resident expert on hellhounds or their bondmates, much less on battle forms and the abilities that manifest during them. We're learning with you as we go."

I nodded as we walked around a small Zen garden section of the larger green space. This area was quiet and seemed removed from the greater garden.

In the center of the small area where we stood, I noticed

the small footpath and koi pond, complete with enormous koi fish swimming lazily in the water.

It took me a few seconds, but I noticed that the trees around the pond were all cherry blossoms. I paused on the stone path we were using to admire the scene.

"This is a traditional zen garden?"

Dex nodded.

"One of the reasons your Director was here as well," he said, stopping to admire the area. "This is a replica of a garden she has at her ancestral home back in Japan. It should look familiar."

"I thought this place looked familiar," I said, recognizing some of the elements present around us. "She helped design this?"

"Not helped," Dex said. "She created it from inception to installation. I merely followed instructions. Your vampire has a keen eye for detail and design."

"I'm not surprised," I said. "Exacting and precise are part of what makes her who she is."

"As expected," Dex said, gazing down into the koi pond. "One doesn't become the leader of the Dark Council by missing details. Which is what I'd like from you right now—details. Elaborate on this power expression."

"Sure," I said, trying to recall the sensation right before Nan knocked the energy from my concentration with a fist. "There was this buildup of energy, and it felt the way a baleful glare looks—if that makes any sense."

"Explain."

"Peaches' eyes get this glare for a few seconds, right before he unleashes his omega beams."

"You're referring to an accumulation of energy?"

"Yes, red energy around and in his eyes builds up right before it shoots out from them."

"These beams, which you call his omega beams, are in

reality his baleful glare, correct?" Dex clarified. "I just want to make sure I have the terms correct."

"Yes."

"Where did you get the term omega beams then?"

I saw Monty roll his eyes and suddenly take an oversized interest in the koi fish swimming in the pond.

"Omega beams are the beams Darkseid fires from his eyes," I said, looking into the blank expression Dex gave me. "They lock onto a target and track them. Do you know who Darkseid is?"

"The dark side of what?" he glanced at Monty. "Do you know what he's going on about with this...dark side? The dark side of what?"

"He's a comic-book villain who fires beams that disintegrate anything they impact," Monty explained. "Actually, as far as explanations go, they describe his creature's baleful glare quite accurately. For someone not familiar with a baleful glare, it makes sense."

"Comic-book villain?" Dex asked, giving me a level-two Clint glint. I have to admit I was impressed. He must have been taking classes from the Morrigan. "Care to stay with us in the real world, boy? We're not fighting comic-book villains. We have our hands full with the real ones."

"Just giving you an explanation of what the energy felt like," I said. "I've never felt anything like it before."

"Hmm," Dex said, rubbing his chin in thought. "It's never been documented before—bondmates sharing baleful glares —but tell me the other properties of the battle form."

I ran down the transformation for him, explaining how I saw Peaches change, and the changes to my own body.

"Let me see your arms," Dex said, pulling my arms forward. "These runes you describe only appear during the battle form?"

I nodded.

"Your hound becomes more muscular and grows?" he asked. "Grows how?"

"Not XL size, not super large," I explained, "but closer to this height." I showed him by placing my hand on the level of my head. "Somewhere between normal and XL."

"Aye, that tracks. Cerberus is an imposing creature, but he's an adult hellhound bonded to a god," Dex said, giving me the once-over. "What about you? Is it just the runes? Or do you grow as well?"

"Hasn't happened yet, but Peaches and this battle form didn't come with a manual," I answered pensively. "Maybe I could grow like him?"

"I hope the only growth you exhibit is in intelligence, boy," Dex said with small smile. "Again, I've never heard of bondmates growing with their hellhounds, and Hades isn't a good example, being a god. Very little that applies to him would apply to you. What else happens?"

"My skin becomes more dense," I said. "I have to assume my bones do, too. Some of the blows Nan gave me should have broken me."

"Denser skin? Probably to match the increased density of your cranial cavity," he said with a straight face. "How did Nan stop this energy that was forming around your eyes?"

"With a fist to my head and a warning that she wasn't having any of that."

He chuckled.

"Crude, but effective."

"So glad that could provide you with a moment of humor."

"Stop being so thin-skinned," he said. "She was actually helping you, and doing it in the fastest way possible. You want to know the quickest way to disrupt a mage while casting?"

"How? Break their fingers to prevent the finger-wiggling?"

"The gestures serve as mnemonic devices," Dex answered, shaking his head. "I worry about you sometimes, boy, I really do. No, the fastest way to disrupt a mage is to do what Nan did to you. A solid strike to the head. Disrupt the brain, and the casting goes to shite."

"Well, she disrupted my brain with extreme force," I said. "Right before she launched me off the roof."

"She launched you off the roof?"

"Yes," I said, holding up two fingers. "Did you *tell* her to beat me to a pulp? You *were* the one who sent her to me, right?"

"Shush for a moment," he said, holding up a finger as if grasping a thought. "I know you're all in your feelings about how Nan pounded on you, but I need you to pay attention to my next question. Do not answer right away, give it some thought first. Ready?"

"Ready," I said warily. "Ask me anything."

"Have you seen, recently, as in after the Evergreen-Gault incident, anything strange in your daily goings-on?" he asked. "By strange, I mean something closer to—"

"Are you serious?" I asked, raising my voice and cutting him off. "Have I seen anything *strange*? Only every time I look in the mirror. Or when I look at my hellhound—did I tell you I have a hellhound? An actual denizen of the Underworld—yes, *that* Underworld, Hades and everything—the place and, get this, the god too!"

"No need to be such an—" he started before he narrowed his eyes at me again and sighed. "Oh, bloody hell, Mo."

He motioned for Monty to stay back. I noticed all of this as if I were a spectator inside my own body, which had gone out of control. I was watching my body react and speak, but somehow I was powerless to stop myself. The words came spilling out.

I wondered if this was what happened when a nervous

breakdown caught up with you. After everything I had encountered lately, I was overdue for one.

"My hellhound is named Peaches," I continued, because for a brief moment it felt like reality was playing a cruel joke on me and it was slowly slipping from my grasp. I didn't understand my reaction. It was as if my brain had gone on autopilot. "No, I didn't name him, thanks for asking, but it's a great name, thank you. He is awesome, yes. Would I consider him strange? Well, you could say that, yes. He can teleport, eat many times his own weight in meat—he prefers pastrami, by the way. He blasts laser beams from his eyes—yes, actual beams of energy—and has a sonic bark that can destroy pretty much anything."

"Simon, he's not mocking..." Monty began.

Dex shook his head and Monty became silent.

"Oh, and there's my bondbrother, Tristan Montague," I said as Dex motioned to Monty to let me speak. "I wouldn't say he's strange, exactly, but he *is* a mage. Does that qualify as strange?"

"It does," Dex said, keeping his voice calm. "Anything else?"

"Anything else?" I answered as my voice increased in volume. "Plenty! I'm just getting started!"

"Please share," Dex said. "I'd like to hear it."

"I can form a magic missile," I said, lowering my voice to conspiratorial tones. "I even took down a plane once with one —you should recall, as it was your suggestion that helped bring down the plane. You were on the plane with me."

"I do recall. I was there."

"Glad to hear your memory is working just fine," I said. "Mine is peachy keen. What is happening to me?"

"Please continue," Dex said. "Something else?"

"I can't believe you're asking me if I've seen something strange," I said, getting my voice under control as I calmed down. "Everything I see, every day I wake up, is something strange. What the hell kind of question is that?"

"Are you done?" Dex asked and waited for me to finish. "Got it all out?"

"For now," I said. "Have I seen anything strange? You've got to be kidding me."

"Done?"

"Yes," I snapped. "I'm done."

"I'm sorry you had to go through that," Dex said apologetically. "It's a side effect of spending unfiltered time with Mo."

"Unfiltered time?"

"Sometimes, she has that effect on people," Dex said. "I thought you wouldn't be as affected, being exposed to Kali and other divine entities, but sometimes Mo just hits someone wrong, and they step into an episode. It's something similar to an anxiety attack, but with more blood and death."

"That could have happened to me?"

"I wouldn't have let it get that far," Dex assured me. "Have you ever heard of the berserker's rage? She was responsible for a fair amount of them. Something to do with getting ready for death and battle. Part of who she is. I don't think she does it intentionally; sometimes it just happens—as if it's some dangerous aura around her."

"Holy hell," I said, sitting on a nearby bench and rubbing the back of my head, which felt like a drum for an angry ogre with a sledgehammer, pounding out a beat with the meanest headache in the existence of man. "I felt like I was losing my mind. One moment, I was there—normal—and the next, your question triggered that entire rant."

"Usually how it goes," Dex said, looking off into the larger garden with a short nod. "That's usually followed by either plenty of sword waving, axe swinging, or orb flinging. Shortly after that, something's getting cut or disintegrated, along with plenty of blood being spilled, and many people dying. It's never pretty."

"This reinforces your theory, Uncle," Monty said as he gestured, and golden runes descended on me to join the heat in my body as my curse worked to correct whatever it was the Morrigan's aura of madness had done to me. "It was almost identical."

"I just didn't expect him to be this affected," Dex said. "This is due to your bond."

"What theory?" I asked, confused. "What's identical?"

"Tristan had a similar episode last night," Dex said, sitting down next to me. "I thought it was due to the fatigue, but now the same thing has happened to you, and I can't assume it's not connected."

"Connected to what?" I asked. "What are you saying?"

He raised a hand and took a deep breath before letting it out.

"Let me finish my question," he said, placing a hand on my shoulder. "I meant if you had seen anything strange, even for us."

"You're going to have to be a bit more specific than that," I said. "Ever since I stepped into this world, strange has lost all its meaning. Can you narrow it down a bit?"

"Yes," he said and glanced at Monty, who nodded back. "I can be somewhat more specific."

"What is going on?" I said, exasperated. "Just say it already. What could be so out of the norm that you would hesitate to just say it?"

"Aye, this is a rare occasion, even for me," he said, rubbing a hand through his hair. "I'm not one to lack words for any occasion. But fair is fair—you deserve a straight question, even if you can't provide a straight answer."

"What does that mean?"

"Simon, listen," Monty said. "Pay close attention."

"That's what I've been doing ever since we stepped into this overgrown forest masquerading as a park," I said, getting angry. "So far, all I'm hearing are things that don't make sense —I mean, *really* don't make sense, which has to be some kind of first for my life."

"Simon, have you seen any dead people?"

"What is this, some kind of trick question?" I asked with a chuckle that sounded more nervous than I wanted. "Of course I've seen dead people. We've all seen dead people."

"Have any of them come back?"

"Come back?" I asked, trying to make sense of the question. "What do you mean, come back?"

"As in, someone you were absolutely certain was dead, but has managed to revisit you, or appear to you," Dex clarified, keeping his voice even and calm. "Anyone from your past, recent or distant? Specifically, someone who was an enemy?"

"Appear to me? Like in a dream? An enemy?"

Dex shook his head, and I could see he was trying to guide me to the subject gently. It was just that my brain was short-circuiting, because despite everything I had experienced, I refused to believe that the dead were now going to start roaming the streets.

"Are you talking about necromancy?" I asked, hoping that's what he meant. "Is there another necromancer loose? Do you mean shamblers?"

"It's something a little more complicated than just necromancy or shamblers," Dex said. "Do you recall your final fight with Gault on Little Island?"

"I do, yes," I said. "What about it? Are you saying Gault is back? No way!" I said with a nervous laugh. "He can't be back. Right?"

"No, no," Dex said, raising his hands. "Gault is gone, period. End of story."

I let out a sigh of relief.

"Good," I said. "I don't understand what you mean. What do dead people have to do with me and my training with Nan? What did Monty go through?"

"Were you using your blade when you fought Nan?"

"Only if I wanted to survive," I said. "She was taking no prisoners. Yes, I was using my blade, or we wouldn't be having this conversation right now."

"I thought as much," Dex said. "And when the energy formed around your eyes?"

"I was still fighting Nan."

"Were you still using Ebonsoul?"

"Yes," I said, stating the obvious. "I told you she was taking no prisoners."

Dex glanced at Monty.

"The blade has to be the catalyst," Dex said. "Your episode happened first and was more pronounced because you carried more of the First Elder Rune."

"That would explain why he hasn't seen anyone," Monty said. "I was carrying the burden of the rune."

"It would be great if you would explain some of this to me," I said. "Who or what did you see?"

"We still don't have all the details," Dex said. "But it seems..." He glanced at Monty. "It seems my nephew is seeing dead people."

ELEVEN

"You *see* dead people?" I asked. "Are you serious? Are you saying we're having a *The Sixth Sense* moment?"

"Yes, except in this scenario we are the little boy, not the dead psychologist," Monty answered. "And you've said you haven't seen anyone from your past who is deceased."

"All the dead from my past have decided to stay dead," I confirmed again as the pounding in my head calmed down. "Who have you seen?"

"I've only gotten brief glimpses, but he bears the semblance of an old sect mate of mine," Monty said. "Someone I was familiar with in my youth, until—"

"Until you had to kill him," Dex said, his expression dark and his words hard. "Taylor was rotten to the core, but he was skilled at hiding his evil. I warned the Elders about that boy the moment I laid eyes on him, and they ignored me until it was too late. By then, the damage had been done."

"What happened?" I asked, dreading to hear the answer. This was the first time I had heard of this friend, and from the sound of things, it wasn't a pleasant story. "What did he do?"

"Cavan Taylor came from a distinguished mage family," Monty said after a short pause to gather his thoughts. "He was an entitled and privileged bully, but his family was influential in the magical community, and he had skill."

"Sounds like a great guy."

"He wasn't," Monty said. "He targeted those less skilled, and oppressed the other sect mates through his family connections."

"And you were friends with this guy?"

"Acquaintances, not friends," Monty corrected. "I thought I could help him, influence him in a positive direction, and be his friend. He had brief moments of kindness, but they were never long enough." He looked away for a moment. "I failed."

"Aye, he was a villain in the making," Dex said, shaking his head. "I told the Elders to expel the little stain, but they feared the repercussions from the other sect families."

"How long ago was this?" I asked.

"This was at the beginning of the Golden Circle, going from mostly a mage school to a mage sect," Monty said. "They depended on the support from those families. The status of becoming a sect was a huge boost in credibility and standing."

"So the Elders looked the other way while this Taylor person terrorized whoever he wanted?" I asked. "What about your dad?"

"My father was only an instructor at the time, with very little influence or say in larger sect matters, and my uncle wasn't exactly favored in the newly formed sect. The Montagues were feared, but not respected."

"Call the kettle black, child," Dex said. "Don't dress it up. Connor was the only respectable Montague in the whole place, aside from my nephew here. As for me"—he unleashed a mischievous grin that bordered on evil—"they truly despised me. I was too strong to confront and too wild to control. I made the Elders' lives a living hell, but they tolerated me until they saw their opportunity."

"To get rid of you?"

"You want to know why I went through the trouble of relocating the Golden Circle?" Dex asked, looking around the green space. "I didn't want this school. I certainly don't need it. What am I going to do with a school?"

"Honestly, I really don't know, besides train more scary battle mages?" I said. "What *are* you going to do with an entire school?"

Dex glared at me.

"It was a rhetorical question, boy," he snapped. "Pay attention."

"Oh."

"I needed to liberate that sect—besides giving myself no end to the thousands of headaches headed my way," he continued. "The Elders, they...they didn't deserve a place like that. A place to shape and form young minds...a place to help the next generation of mages to grow."

"They had stopped creating battle mages," Monty said. "Shortly after I left, the battle mage curriculum was discontinued."

"Imagine that," Dex said. "The Golden Circle, the most prestigious school of battle magic, relegated to a cesspool of old men trying to cling to power."

"Why did they stop teaching battle magic?"

"The Elders were corrupt, but they were also cunning and intelligent," Monty said. "If you want to hold onto your position, the last thing you do is train new mages who could challenge, or even remove you. The threat was removed—no more battle magic was taught."

"It was after the war," Dex said. "Who needs battle mages in a time of peace? They convinced the other sects it was the right path and defanged the magical community. Connor didn't see the danger, and by the time he did...it was too late."

"This was the *only* school?" I asked. "Battle magic isn't taught in any of the other sects?"

"There are disciplines, yes," Monty said. "I'm sure you would argue that Quan is an excellent fighter, but as a White Phoenix, she is a healer first and a fighter second."

"The Golden Circle was created to constantly seek out the last one," Dex said. "It was a never-ending mission."

"The last one?"

"Aye, when you've walked as many killing fields as I have, you recognize the last one almost immediately," Dex said. "They're devilishly hard to kill."

I looked at Monty with the question in my eyes.

"In English?" I asked. "The last one of what?"

"On any given battlefield, with any given battle force, this formula has been, with surprising accuracy, replicated time and time again."

Typical mage answer.

"Sounds downright scientific and cryptic as hell," I said, getting frustrated. "The last one of what?"

"I'll answer your question with one of my own," Dex said, facing me, his expression a mixture of seriousness and humor. "Once you answer me, you'll have your answer."

"Why would I ever expect a straight answer?" I said, throwing a hand up. "What was I thinking?"

"You really should know better," Dex said with a small chuckle. "Here is the question: Between Peanut and Cecelia, which one is the last one?"

"Am I having another minor nervous breakdown? The last one of what?"

"Remind him," Dex said, looking at Monty. "He knows. He's just being pigheaded."

"I'm not—" I started.

Dex raised a hand, asking for silence, and pointed at Monty.

Monty took a deep breath and let it out slowly, before adjusting the sleeves of his jacket. I grew wary, because telling Monty to remind me sounded like an instruction to have Monty unleash some orbs in my direction.

"You have a group of one hundred mages," Monty began, entering mage professor mode. "A conflict arises and they must go to battle. Following so far?"

He gestured and a swarm of small, golden orbs formed between us. I nodded, but kept my guard up slightly, in case Dex decided this was a good moment to give my head a memory-jarring *thump*.

"Out of those hundred," Monty continued, waving a hand, causing a group to turn blue, "ten shouldn't even be there." Another hand wave and most of them turned red. "Sadly, eighty...eighty are just targets."

He glanced over at Dex, who nodded as Monty made another gesture, turning the remaining orbs a brighter gold, with one of them being brighter than all the rest. "Nine are the real fighters, and we are lucky to have them, for they make the battle. Ah, but one,"—Monty pointed at the brightest orb—"the last one, is the warrior, and he will bring the others back."

With another wave of his hand, the orbs vanished.

"Heraclitus," Dex said, anger lacing his words. "The Golden Circle was formed to find that last one. They forgot what this place was for. They failed those mages. They created a place where a mage like Oliver...a mage like Oliver could grow, thrive, and kill."

"Also, you just wanted to make them suffer," Monty added matter-of-factly. "You stole...relocated, an entire sect, Uncle, without a Council meeting, without so much as a note informing the Elders what was going to happen. You gave them no warning whatsoever."

"Never, ever, warn your enemies," Dex spat. "Mark my words, they were, and still are, my enemies... and yours, too, nephew."

"I'm aware," Monty said. "And you wonder why they hate you so?"

"I don't wonder," Dex said, "and I don't care. Strong, what's your answer? Peanut or Cecelia?"

"Cecelia definitely qualifies as gifted," I said. "She has power and is learning how to use it. Olga wasn't overly pleased about the new ice makeover she gave the Moscow."

"I heard," Dex said with a chuckle before nodding. "She has great potential."

"But Peanut, honestly? Peanut concerns me."

"Aye," Dex said, rubbing his chin as he gazed off into the distance. "Tell me why?"

"She has power."

"Aye, that she does."

"But there's more... She doesn't fear her power like Cece does," I said as the realization surfaced. "She has a strong moral compass, which is good, but I wouldn't want her as an enemy."

"The child has faced death threats many times over her short life," Dex said. "It's not right, and we can't change her past, but we can help shape her future. It doesn't have to be all violence and death."

"She seems like she could really be a joint product of you —as the Harbinger—and the Morrigan, but the scary Badb Catha aspect of her."

Dex shuddered.

"That's quite a sobering thought," he said as Monty stared at me. "Not entirely wrong, but she's not that dangerous."

"If I had to choose, I would say Peanut—with training.

The way she is now, I'm not so sure she would or could bring everyone back," I said. "She's not that dangerous, not yet."

"Yet," he admitted. "The correct answer is that they can both be the last one, each in their own way. They both have strengths and weaknesses which can work against them individually, but together, and trained properly...aye, they would be a sight to behold. Maybe when they're older, I'll let them pay the Elders a disciplinary visit."

"You wouldn't," Monty said, surprised. "No one would deserve a visit like that."

"Ach, it would serve them right," Dex said with a wave of his hand. "They were too cowardly to face me in a Duel of Erasure, and went after you instead—you were still a pup."

"A Duel of Erasure?" I asked. "Does that mean what I think it means?"

Monty nodded.

"The loser of the duel has their abilities erased, permanently," Monty explained. "They go from being a mage to—if they are fortunate—teaching magic theory in one of the larger sects. In a sect like the Golden Circle—"

"It's a death sentence," Dex finished. "What good is theory alone to a battle mage? May as well send him into battle with a notebook and a pen, against swords and orbs."

"That does sound like a death sentence," I said. "Couldn't they share their knowledge, and help the next group of battle mages?"

"Nay, in battle magic, theory and practice are married—linked as one. The Elders feared they would lose their positions of prestige and power if they faced me. Truth is, they were no different than Taylor; they only hid it better, until they didn't."

"The Elders threatened my uncle with my expulsion if he didn't leave the sect and all sect business," Monty continued. "Not only would they tarnish me with expulsion, they would prevent any shifts of ascension. They would blacklist me."

"They could do that?"

"In the beginning of the transition, they could," Monty said, glancing at Dex, who smiled as he shook his head. "Later on, certain interested parties changed the sect rules to prevent that kind of control and manipulation."

"Isn't that what sort of happened to you anyway?" I asked. "It's not like the sects are in love with you"—I glanced at Dex —"or any Montague, these days."

"True," Monty admitted. "But I'm not an apprentice mage and am no longer subject to their authority. As for my uncle, he will never change, and has recently decided to relieve them of their entire sect. If they disliked him before, they absolutely loathe him now. It's just more of the same."

"I'm not losing any sleep over it," Dex added. "Let the cowards come at me. I wish they would."

"Anyway, they forced my uncle away for a time, and during that time, Taylor, with the backing of some of the Elders grew in prominence and cruelty."

"They let him run loose?" I asked. "Unchecked?"

"Remember, he was influential and skilled as a mage," Monty said. "They curried favor with his family, and Taylor did whatever he wanted in the Golden Circle."

"Sounds like a recipe for disaster."

"He should have left well enough alone," Dex said, "though I'm not saying he'd still be here today if he had. Mages of his ilk are born twisted, seeking out darkness from an early age, but he could've had a chance. Sometimes that's all you need."

"Taylor had taken to torturing some of the lower sect mates," Monty said. "At first it was harmless pranks, typical hazing. Nothing serious."

"It changed, didn't it?" I asked. "Bullies like him never

stay low-stakes for long. The thrill isn't there; it's in the danger, with seeing how far and how much they can get away with, without consequence."

Monty nodded.

"Taylor, together with his little group of friends, had targeted some of the lower-skilled mages and made their lives a living hell. One day, they went too far, and I confronted him. I thought he would be open to reason, that he would listen to my advice, based on our earlier friendship, despite the fact that it was strained at the time."

"Let me guess—he told you to take a walk," I said. "He was going to do whatever he wanted, and you weren't going to stop him."

"More or less," Monty said. "So I took matters into my own hands."

TWELVE

"You killed him?"

"Simon, really?" Monty asked, shaking his head. "This was a sect of young mages, not the outer rings of the Moving Market."

"Hey," I said, raising my hand in surrender. "How am I supposed to know what happens in mage sects? For all I know, you had death matches after study hall every Thursday."

Monty shook his head and sighed.

Dex shook his head too, the small smile on his face filled with sadness.

"My nephew tried to reason with him," Dex said. "Taylor wasn't always twisted, but he was the special project of one of the Elders who used and manipulated him—an Elder seeking more power and seeing young Taylor as the way to gain it. Taylor was standing at a crossroads; this Elder pushed him towards darkness."

"Elder Gwell," Monty said. "He turned Taylor against me. Told him I was plotting to have him erased and expelled from the school."

"Taylor believed him?"

"We were young, impressionable mages. Gwell was an adult and an Elder," Monty said. "Taylor believed him. Gwell used the animosity against my uncle as leverage."

Monty's expression was one of pain as he recalled the memory.

"What did you do?"

"Taylor was enraged at the thought of my plotting against him, and confronted me," Monty said, his gaze distant, recalling the memory. "I tried to de-escalate the situation. I denied it, but Elder Gwell had Taylor completely convinced. There was no reasoning with him. Taylor issued a Black Duel. I had to respond."

"A Black Duel?" I asked. "Let me guess, it's worse than a Duel of Erasure?"

"Black Duels can only occur between established mages," Dex said. "Not the wet-behind-the-ears pups still studying in a sect. It never should have been allowed, and the Elders knew that."

"A Black Duel leaves only one mage standing," Monty clarified. "Sometimes neither, if both die from the wounds inflicted. They are banned, now, and were rare even in my youth. Occasionally, one would happen on the battlefield, but during the war, mages were too important to sacrifice in duels. The practice was ended."

"Good riddance too," Dex added. "Duels happen to be one of the most idiotic ways to throw your life away. Dying for pride and honor is pointless, save one scenario."

"There's a scenario where it's okay to throw your life away?"

"Don't be daft," Dex said with a growl. "That's never okay. But proxy duels, where mages voluntarily represent countries or entire sects, serve a purpose. Better to lose one or two than thousands or hundreds of thousands."

I nodded my understanding.

"Couldn't you petition to another Elder, or submit a formal protest?" I asked. "You *had* to participate in this Black Duel?"

"Elder Gwell was one of the highest ranking Elders in the sect, and did I mention that the Montagues weren't particularly liked?"

"You may have mentioned that a few times, yes," I said. "Since you're here telling me this story, I'm guessing you won the duel."

"No," Monty said. "The duel never happened. Taylor and Elder Gwell attacked me before the appointed day. They were determined to end me."

"What? What happened?"

"I realized something was off a few days before the appointed day," Monty said as we continued down the stone path. "Taylor had become overly friendly, more so than usual. Even Gwell had been speaking kindly to me."

"Red flags," I said. "To lull you into a false sense of security."

"Indeed," Monty said. "It's clearer now, with the benefit of hindsight and experience."

"What did they try and do?"

"The receiver of the duel challenge can set the weapons and casts," Monty said. "Under the guise of trying to make the duel fair, Taylor, and later on Gwell, convinced me that it would be in my best interests to restrict the casts to the current curriculum focus. After some convincing, I agreed... much to my detriment."

"That sounds bad," I said. "Why does that sound bad?"

"Because it was," Monty said. "Before I agreed, I researched what Taylor had been currently studying. According to the program, he was in the midst of life-extension studies."

"He was studying how to get old? That sounds harmless."

"Not quite. He was studying how not to die on a battle-field, so as to inflict death on others," Monty corrected. "It was a branch of study in his particular discipline that made magic users of his type particularly dangerous."

"I take that back. That sounds incredibly harmful," I said, realizing the danger of that body of knowledge. "What exactly was Taylor's discipline?"

"He was a specific type of necromancer, one with a narrow focus," Monty said. "He was a deathcaster."

"Like Fel Sepsis?"

"Sephtis," he corrected. "Technically correct; they were both necromancers, but Fel Sephtis became a revenant. I have no idea what Taylor has become, or if it even is the real Taylor. In any case, a deathcaster is a rare and highly special-ized type of necromancer."

"What—he deals in *extra* death?"

Monty only gave me a look. Dex growled nearby, convincing me that it was currently safer to stand a few feet away from the old mage.

"When we were at war, the deathcasters were the equiva-lent of a special-operations group of one. They were the mages they occasionally put on the front lines, just to scare the bravado out of the enemy."

"Shit, that sounds bad."

"It was. But if he had been currently studying life-exten-sion techniques, I was safe—or so I thought."

"He wasn't currently studying life-extension techniques, was he?"

"No, he had been currently immersed in the study of targeted necrotic dissolution," Monty said. "Remote disinte-gration, though I didn't know this at the time."

"What had you been studying?"

"Offensive teleportation," he said. "I had been deceived.

Gwell had switched Taylor's training program, knowing I would do my due diligence and research the current materials of study."

"Everyone thought you were dead, didn't they?"

He nodded.

"And I would have been, if it hadn't been for my uncle," he said, glancing at Dex. "As far as Gwell, Taylor, or anyone knew, teleportation—even offensive teleportation—meant using teleportation circles to evade your opponent. They were a means of escape."

"That makes sense," I said. "Offensive teleports means you can't catch me. You can't beat what you can't hit."

"My uncle had created a different application for them," he said. "Something far more deadly—something he showed me."

THIRTEEN

I recalled all the times I had seen Dex use teleportation circles in unconventional ways, throwing them around as weapons. I could see teleportation circles as dangerous, at least in his hands.

"He showed you how to use them as real weapons," I said. "Not just for evasion."

"I didn't want to," Dex said as we stopped at a small bridge. The sound of birds singing filled the air. I didn't recognize the song, but it made the park-forest feel tranquil. "If I hadn't, they would've killed him. We protect the family."

"Gwell was attempting to get his vengeance on you by trying to eliminate Monty," I said. "You did the right thing."

"Ach, even though duels are a colossal waste, the right thing would've been for that coward to face me in mortal combat," Dex said, looking down at the small brook that ran under the bridge, lost in his own thoughts. "Against my better judgment, I would have accepted *that* duel. Instead, he pitted two children against each other—poisoning the mind of one, and placing the other in an impossible position."

"Why couldn't you just leave?" I asked, looking at Monty. "Wasn't that an option? Just get up and go?"

"Go where? The Golden Circle was my home," Monty said, shaking his head. "Leaving wasn't an option. Besides, there were other considerations. Gwell needed to be stopped, Taylor was a bully and would become worse if he wasn't stopped, and my family name...my family's name was at stake."

"I get stopping Gwell and stomping Taylor," I said. "I don't understand the family name part. Why was that so important?"

"I didn't want to be feared any longer," Monty said, glancing at Dex before continuing. "Do you know what it's like to enter school and have no friends? No one willing to associate with you, not because of anything you've done, but because of your family name? Something completely out of your control?"

"No, I don't," I answered honestly. "The Strong name doesn't have that kind of rep where I come from. These days, I just let them see Peaches first, I make sure he smiles, and let them form whatever opinions they want. They're usually wrong, but still, a little fear is a good thing."

Dex chuckled.

"Agreed, though I'd say the name Simon Strong has some weight to it now," Dex said. "But the lad was right; he couldn't leave and he couldn't back down. He was trapped, so I armed him as best as I could—with Connor's blessing."

"Your dad knew?"

Monty nodded.

"My father was the consummate politician," Monty said. "He could outplay and outmaneuver the Elders when it came to sect politics, but he didn't have enough support or influence to stop the duel outright, not yet."

"Sect politics became the end of him," Dex said, his

expression dark as we continued through the park. "He gave as good as he got, right up to the end. My brother was brilliant and gifted. He only had one flaw."

"Which was?"

"He was too good, and always chose to see only the good in others," Dex said. "In my world, that way of being gets you an early grave, as it did him."

"We shouldn't see the good in others?" I asked. "You do realize not *everyone* is out to destroy us?"

"I didn't say that, *boy*," Dex said with the last word being accompanied and emphasized with a head *thwack*. "I said you can't see *only* the good. We all have darkness inside, some more than others, but it's there. Choosing not to see it is... shortsighted, and foolish. Connor was my brother and I loved him to death, but he could be a shortsighted fool. At least in this he listened to me. In this situation, he listened to reason."

"What did he do?"

"He couldn't stop the duel, so he did the next best thing," Monty continued. "He managed an extension to move the date of the duel."

"He delayed it?"

"Aye, said the lad here needed time to prepare," Dex said, "and shipped him off to me for a few months, where I taught him the basic floating teleport and gave him an amplifier to be able to execute it. Do you still have it?"

Monty nodded.

"It's secure with Erik at the Hellfire Club," Monty said. "That artifact is too volatile to keep outside of a neutralizing field. Hellfire has several which were ideal."

"Too volatile?" I asked confused. "What kind of artifact?"

"Tristan wasn't strong enough to execute a floating teleport at the time, not without the shunting disc artifact."

"The what and a what?" I asked. "What is a floating teleport?"

"This," Dex said and formed a large green circle in the air in front of us. "Hold on."

"Hold on?" I asked, looking around. "Hold on to what? Dex what are you—?"

With a sideways slash of his arm, the circle collided with me, and the park vanished—only it didn't *really* vanish, but rather I was the one who had moved. I looked around and found myself floating above a cloud bank. The off-angle light of whatever passed for the sun in this place was creating an assortment of reds, oranges, pinks, and deep yellows.

The light looked amazing as it bounced off the clouds.

It was incredible for all of two seconds, until I realized I was hovering an impossible distance above the park, which appeared to be a small patch of grass below me, as a miniature Dex and Monty looked up at me.

Fear gripped me immediately as I realized how high up I was.

"Dex!" I yelled as gravity took hold and I began falling. "DEX!"

"Don't panic!" Dex called out. "You'll be right down!"

"Why would I panic?" I muttered to myself as I picked up speed and dropped. "I'm only going to end up as a bloody, broken puddle of bits when I hit the ground. He couldn't have just *explained* the concept? He had to launch me into the stratosphere?"

I looked around again and caught movement out of the corner of my eye—not that I could do anything about it. Another green circle raced under me. I dropped into it, and a second later, found myself standing in front of Dex and Monty back in the park, standing completely still.

"The floating teleport," Dex said with a slight bow. "One

of the most unconventional ways to use a teleportation circle ever discovered."

"You... you could have just told me," I said as I stumbled over to a nearby bench. "It's amazing, really."

"Aye," Dex said. "I could have explained it, but this was simpler. Don't you think?"

"I think my stomach is going to have trouble reuniting with the rest of my body after that explanation, that's what I think. It's impressive, but I don't see it as a weapon. Unless you use it to scare opponents to death."

"That's because you're lacking perspective," he said, forming another, smaller, circle, this one about three inches in size. "Allow me to show you."

"You just did! Thanks!" I said, raising my hands. "You don't need to show me anything more. I believe you—it's a weapon, a really effective weapon!"

"Calm down, boy," Dex said with a smile. "And stop being so skittish. You've faced gods trying to break you; I'm just a harmless, old man with a tiny teleportation circle."

"No one believes any part of you is harmless," I protested. "That's just a flat-out lie."

"Shush," he said and looked around. "I have to make sure she isn't around, or she'll have my hide if she finds out I damaged her park."

"Who?" I asked, looking around. "Who would have your hide?"

"Who else? Mo."

"Oh," I said, looking around the park. "She likes this park, does she?"

"This place is known as the Morrigan's Grove," he said, keeping his voice low. "She designed the entire place and allowed some small outside influences to make it diverse, but make no mistake, this is *her* park. She does not tolerate damage to *her* park."

"I didn't know."

"She is quite the creator, you know," he said, letting the small teleportation circle turn in his hand. "Surprised me several times."

"Who would've thought?" I said. "Especially from a death goddess."

"True. Along with your vampire, they have transformed many aspects of the school grounds, but Mo is the creative force behind the entire school. Now, watch."

He gestured, and the small teleportation circle raced over towards one of the thicker trees a few feet away, turning on its side, and becoming perpendicular to the tree as it closed.

It impacted silently into the side of the tree, carving out a smooth, three-inch wide tunnel throughout the entire thickness of the tree as it kept moving forward.

The tree didn't even slow it down.

"Was that the—?"

He walked me over to the tree and motioned for me to look through the freshly carved-out tunnel. I saw straight through the tree and into Dex's face as he walked over to the other side to gaze through the hole he had made.

"The floating teleport," he said with a nod through the tree. "Now imagine something like that, not quite as refined, but still fairly powerful, hitting a body."

"It didn't even slow it down," I said. "It's not operating under normal laws of physics, is it?"

"Good catch," Dex said. "The real explanation is something my nephew or Ziller would love to take three hours to explain. I'll make it short: it works by teleporting whatever it encounters...away."

"That would be a brutal attack," I said, seeing the implications. "The target wouldn't know what hit them until it was too late."

I glanced at Monty.

"Is that what happened?" I continued. "You used *that* on Taylor?"

"No," Monty said as we kept moving. I saw Dex gesture and return the tree to its earlier state, patting it with a few whispered words and a few subtle looks to the sides, before moving on to catch up with us. "I knew Taylor was being manipulated by Gwell, so I did the most logical thing—or at least it was logical to my young mind at the time."

"You ran and found stronger mages to kick their asses after you discovered the deception," I said, "avoiding the entire conflict and flexing your newfound diplomacy skills?"

"No," he said, surprised. "Why would I do that?"

"You said *logical*," I answered. "I forgot you were referring to mage logic. Continue."

"Besides, I lacked diplomacy skills at the time."

"At the time?" I said incredulously. "It's not like you're a top-level mage diplomat now, you know. I'm not recalling you resolving our near-death conflicts with the eloquence of your words."

"Irrelevant."

"Pretty relevant when our lives depend on these non-existent diplomatic skills of yours. Just saying."

"In any case, I issued a challenge of my own," Monty said. "I challenged Gwell."

"The Elder? You challenged the *Elder?*"

"Dueling Taylor was the same as dueling Gwell," Monty explained. "Taylor was a proxy being controlled by the Elder. I reasoned that the best way to resolve this dilemma was to attack the source."

"That sounds like such a bad idea."

"The worst," Dex added. "Which, for the record, I did *not* tell him to do. I told him to end Taylor. My beneficent nephew disagreed with me and thought Taylor could still be redeemed. He just needed—what was it you said he needed?

—ah yes, 'an understanding ear and the solid shoulder of friendship to lean on.' That was it."

"I was wrong," Monty said. "Gwell accepted my challenge even though he shouldn't have, but instructed Taylor to attack me first."

"Taylor attacked?"

Monty nodded. "A few days after I returned from my uncle's home, pretending to be my friend, he struck," he said. "I was under the impression he would try some kind of life-altering cast on me based on the life-extension casts."

"He tried to alter your life, right and proper," Dex said, shaking his head. "By ending it, then and there."

"What did you do?"

"Offensive teleportation," Monty said. "I evaded his initial attack and unleashed one of my own, similar to what you just saw my uncle do to that tree. In fact, it was an identical attack."

"And punched a hole through Taylor," I said with a nod of certainty. "It's what I would've done, it's what he deserved. Especially if he tried to disintegrate—"

"No, I sent the circle at Gwell," Monty said cutting me off. "I didn't attack Taylor."

"You—what?"

"*Gwell* was the source, not Taylor," Monty said. "He was the corruption. He had Taylor all twisted. I thought if I could stop him, Taylor would see reason. I didn't realize it was too late for Taylor."

"Gwell called out for assistance and Taylor being a young and naive mage thought he could stop the floating teleport," Dex said. "He stood in front of Elder Gwell and tried to cast a lattice of dispersion, a shield to stop the circle."

"It didn't work, did it?"

"No," Dex said, shaking his head. "The floating teleport is my own creation. It's designed to be nearly unstoppable. Only

Mo has managed to slow it down—not stop it, mind you, but slow it down enough to deflect it. And she had to work to do even that. They never stood a chance."

"My attack cut through the both of them," Monty said. "They died where they stood."

"I don't understand," I said. "If your floating teleport killed them both, why are you now seeing Taylor? How is he back? He's dead."

"An excellent question," Dex said. "That's where you and your blade come in."

FOURTEEN

"Me and my blade?" I asked. "I don't follow."

"Think back to your battle with Gault," Dex said.

"Which one? We clashed a few times."

Dex gave me a withering stare.

"The last one," he said. "You remember—the one where you should've been dead a few times over."

"Oh, *that* one. It's a little fuzzy, but I think I can remember it."

"Try real hard," Dex said. "Let's go over the details you recall, and some you may have forgotten."

"Do we have to?" I asked with a wince. "It wasn't one of my better battles."

"Any fight you can walk away from is a good one," Dex said. "That being said, your performance stank. You were full of openings and didn't exploit any of Gault's weaknesses."

"We were facing a *Keeper*," I protested. "This wasn't some low-level mage. Gault wasn't running a training exercise—he wanted to unleash entropy."

"And your job was simple," Dex replied. "You had to stop him from doing that."

"We did," I snapped. "It may have been sloppy, but it got done, and we're here to tell the tale. I call that a win. Don't you?"

"There's something to be said for elegance in methodology, boy," he said. "What does it matter if you win the battle and lose the war?"

"I don't understand," I said, not following. "We beat him. We stopped Gault and what he wanted to do. We won."

"Aye, but something much worse may have been triggered," he said, as he led us to one of the smaller training circles on the other side of the park. "Let's go over the battle."

"Fine," I said, not enjoying where this conversation was going. "Let's review... Wait, how are you going to review? You weren't even there."

"I was," Dex said. "Did you really think I was going to leave the outcome of this conflict to you two? What do you take me for, a madman?"

"Well..."

"Rhetorical, boy."

"Right, sorry."

"Anyway, I had Herk on site, and I was moving across the field, too fast for you—or anyone, really—to notice. What do you recall?"

I let my thoughts take me back to Little Island.

"I no longer had the catalyst," I said. "Facing Gault directly was off the table. He would blast me to dust if I tried to go up against him directly. He was too strong."

"Wise call," Dex said, with a nod. "You were no match for him with the catalyst, less so without. Continue."

"My job was to hold Gault's forces at the footbridge," I said, remembering the plan. "Hold them off long enough to give Monty an opening."

"Aye, that's why I sent the Echelon."

"*You* sent the Echelon?"

"They told you as much, boy," Dex said. "Weren't you paying attention?"

"I was a little busy trying not to die with thralls, ogres, trollgres, and their assorted friends," I shot back. "Excuse me if I may have been a bit distracted."

"Never mind. The battle wasn't at the footbridge, and the Echelon performed admirably as always," Dex said. "Those women are impressive."

"Scary is what they are," I said. "They shredded everything on the footbridge. That whole thing about me becoming the tip of the spear—was that you?"

"Was that me...what?"

"Was that your idea? My becoming the tip of the spear?"

"You want to know if I formulated a plan to stop a Keeper who wanted to unleash entropy on...*everything*, and that in creating this plan, my secret weapon—my *ultimate* weapon to stop a Keeper—was a half-baked immortal and his ever-hungry bondmate pup of a hellhound? That's what you're asking?"

"Well, when you put it that way, never mind," I said, chastised. "Peaches and I were going to be the tip of the spear when we got the signal."

"You did well in holding them off," Dex said. "I especially enjoyed your moments with the trollgres."

"I didn't."

"I know. In that moment, you fought well and held your own against a trollgre," Dex replied. "Not an easy feat. Something important happened there, though. Do you remember?"

I nodded.

"I buried Ebonsoul into the trollgre and it exploded."

Dex nodded.

"The catalyst of the First Elder Rune," he said, as he

crouched down and touched the edge of the circle we stood in. Violet energy raced along the interior of the large circle. "Your blade still had part of the catalyst."

"A remnant of the rune bonded to Ebonsoul."

"Who told you this?" Dex asked, suddenly alarmed. "That's what happened, but there was no way for you to possess this knowledge. Tristan?"

"Ebonsoul," I said, and explained what had been happening with my blade—or more accurately the sentient being inside my blade, Izanami, who was trying to get extra friendly with me. "It's under control."

"It better be, or this is going to get so much worse," he said. "It does explain much. Proceed. You are getting to the heart of this matter."

"Why not just tell me?" I asked, getting frustrated. "It would be faster and easier if you just told me."

"It would, but you would miss key aspects you must understand," he said. "Telling you is not the same as you coming to the realization on your own. Stop fighting the process. Keep going."

I groaned and gathered my thoughts.

"The Darkanists attacked by opening portals, so I let Peaches convince them that was a bad idea," I said, with a smile at the memory. "That's when Vi and the rest of the Nightwing arrived."

Dex nodded.

"Phase two," Dex said. "It was time for you to go."

"I skirmished with some more Darkanists, but TK and LD...well, they unleashed their inner TK and LD, and crushed everything," I said. "I'm really glad they're on our side."

"Me too, boy, me too," Dex said with a nod. "TK gave you a message. Did you happen to catch it?"

"A message?" I asked. "Was this before the Darkanists were trying to bury their blades into me, or after?"

"No matter," Dex said, waving my words away. "Continue."

"I remember sparing the last Darkanist, Henderson," I said as Dex nodded. "That's when I saw Monty and Lotus fighting Gault."

"They were losing. You all were," Dex said. "He had them trapped."

"He was going to kill them, to get the First Elder Rune," I said, remembering the moment vividly. "That was when I tried the battle form, but it didn't really work."

"You weren't ready," Dex said. "But it was a good attempt. Your pup managed to give you the push you needed, and Lotus held a surprise for the Keeper. She even surprised me."

"Even with all of that, we were failing," I said. "Gault was too strong."

"What stopped him?"

I didn't answer right away as I replayed the sequence in my mind. I remembered Lotus screaming, stripping Ebonsoul from my grip as she lunged at Gault, burying my blade in his chest.

I saw the white runes along the blade's length erupt with white light as the same white light erupted in Lotus, which transformed into a tether of golden-white energy between them.

Then the darkness—which spread everywhere.

I explained this all to Dex, who nodded as I spoke.

"*Tempus edax rerum*," Monty said. "Time is the devourer of all things."

"Those words," I said as the realization hit me. "That's what TK said. Time was a factor in this."

"It still is," Dex said. "Tell me what happened."

"Yes," Monty said. "Lotus delayed the entropic dissolution, powered by the First Elder Rune. Ebonsoul activated the siphon."

"But you were still connected to the First Elder Rune," Dex said. "The catalyst of which had bonded to Ebonsoul."

"That means that the siphon the blade activated was different this time. This time, it was—"

"*Necrotic*," I said, trying to follow the connection before the headache threatening to turn my brain to mush succeeded. "Ebonsoul is a necrotic seraph, which makes the siphon a necrotic siphon? What does that even mean?"

"It means your blade—through the connection you and my nephew had with the First Elder Rune, and influenced by the entropic darkness Gault had summoned—unleashed a necrotic tether."

"A necrotic tether?"

"Think of it as a door to the dead," Dex said, simplifying it for me. "A doorway that allows the dead to travel to our plane. Nasty stuff."

"That sounds like something we want to avoid," I said slowly. "A tether to what...exactly? Can all the dead access this doorway?"

"Just how hard did Nan hit you earlier?" Dex asked, staring at me. "Of course not. The dead, in this case, have to possess some form of connection to you or Tristan."

"Like this Taylor person?"

"Exactly," Dex said. "In Tristan's case, it seems to be Taylor. In your case...I don't know, but I'm not eager to find out. It may be that Taylor is connected to the both of you somehow, or connected to you through my nephew. I'm not a necromancer. You need a specialist."

"Wait, are you saying someone or something from my past, something dead, is going to start paying me a visit?"

"I don't know," Dex said as he touched some of the symbols around the circle. "I'm sending you to a good friend of mine. Someone who may have answers to undo this curse."

"Curse?" I said, surprised. "You didn't say anything about a curse. We're cursed?"

"What do you think this is, boy?" Dex asked, giving me a look that told me I really needed to keep up. "A blessing? Your blade was involved in the death of a Keeper, something that shouldn't have been possible."

"How?" I asked. "How did it happen?"

"You're not paying attention," Dex said, gesturing with a hand and forming another large green circle. "It shouldn't have happened in the first place."

"But it did," I said. "Lotus had something to do with this, too."

"She facilitated the necrotic siphon when she attacked Gault with Ebonsoul," Monty said. "She created and opened the door, but the connection pre-existed her actions."

Dex nodded and rubbed his chin.

"That's likely," he said. "I don't know, but my best guess? You take a necrotic blade, throw in the First Elder Rune and catalyst, unleash an ample dose of entropic darkness, couple it with a dash of Keeper power, and you get yourself a door to the dead and the attention of something that may or may not be Taylor."

"That sounds like a recipe for disaster," I said. "How do we access this door?"

"From the little I know, if it's what I think it is, you have to walk a corpse road," Dex said. "And you can't take too long. If my nephew is accurate in what he's seen, this door is currently open, and opening wider, but—I'm going to say this again, slowly for the dense of skull—I don't know for certain. I'm not a necromancer."

"What about the Morrigan?" I suggested. "Maybe she knows—?"

"No," Dex said, cutting me off immediately. "She *cannot* help you with this. More than that, you do not *want* her help with this. Believe me on this, boy. The Morrigan is not your answer. Not now, not ever. You don't understand what getting her involved in this would mean. Say it."

"I *don't* understand."

"Exactly, you *don't* understand—but you will in time, and when you do, you'll thank me," he said as he flicked his wrist, disappearing the circle. A few seconds later, the circle reformed next to me, and Peaches was sitting in the middle of it. He was currently sporting an assortment of pink and lilac ribbons braided into his fur and hanging behind his ears. "No time for pleasantries. I brought your hellhound."

"No time for pleasantries?" I said, staring at my hellhound and his ribbon accessories. "We just took the uber-scenic route through Morrigan's Grove, and now we're in a rush?"

"That wasn't the scenic route," Dex said, touching other parts of the circle and watching them shift and transform into different symbols. "That was *the* path to *this* specific circle. There was no other way to get here."

I looked down at the circle we stood in.

FIFTEEN

"Oh," I said. "I thought the trip through the park was just a way to kill time."

"Don't be daft, child," Dex said, touching a few more symbols. "This circle is unique, it's interplanar, and will take you to the home of an old friend, but no one can see you arrive. That takes work. I have to send you there the round-about way."

"Why can't anyone see us arrive?" I asked. "Is this friend of yours wanted or something?"

"Wanted is a strong word," Dex said, touching more symbols and rotating others. "It's probably closer to unwanted, but he is an expert on all forms of necromancy, and is an advanced mage in several disciplines. He can help you with this issue."

"He's a criminal?" I asked, narrowing my eyes at Dex. "You're sending us to a criminal?"

"Criminal has such a negative connotation," Dex said with a shrug. "His views don't always align with the authorities on his plane or, those on several others, for that matter. Besides, you're not there to sightsee. First step, you get there; second step, you find Anu; and third step, you get out. You make the time between the first and third steps as short as possible."

"Because he's not a criminal who is wanted by the authorities of his plane," I said. "You just think it's best we don't spend much time there...for our health. Right?"

"Especially for your health," he said. "I'll try to get you as close as I can, but Anu never stays in one place too long. If you run into the Sun Council—you'll notice them by the sun design on their robes and the nasty attitude—say as little as possible and, whatever you do, do not mention Anu."

"Because he's not exactly wanted," I said, realizing what a bad idea this was. "Let me guess, he's not really bad, he's just misunderstood."

"Oh no, he's about as bad as they come," Dex said with a chuckle, "but he's *my* friend, and he will help you with this."

"Why can't you bring him here?" I asked. "Why do you need to send us there?"

"Anu is too powerful for me to just bring here," Dex replied, crouching down to the ground and slightly adjusting another few symbols. "Then there's the matter of my not knowing exactly where he is. I have his general location, but you're going to have to find his exact location."

"This is insane."

"This is your best shot," Dex said with a tight smile. "Your last best shot was named Orethe. I seem to recall that she's permanently unavailable."

"Shit."

"You're both in a mountain of it, if this is what I think it is," he said and waved me quiet. "Now, hush and let me concentrate. If I don't get these symbols right, finding Anu will be the least of your problems. The plane of Kengir is immense. One miscalculation, and you'll end up in an ocean of sand, hundreds of miles from any civilization."

"Kengir?" Monty said. "This circle is taking us to Kengir? I thought that place was impossible to find?"

"It is," Dex said with a growl. "Especially if you keep interrupting me while I'm inscribing the runic locators for the teleportation circle. Do either of you know how to get there?"

I remained silent and Monty shook his head.

"No?" Dex asked. "Then perhaps you can maintain this attitude of silence while I finish drawing this circle? Is that within the realm of possibility?"

"Completely," I said "We'll keep quiet, right, Monty?"

"Absolutely," Monty said, his voice serious, as he slipped into professor mode and turned in my direction. "Simon, did you know that Professor Ziller posits several theories that prove that the denizens of the plane of Kengir are thought to be the original Sumerians? They—"

"Over there!" Dex said, raising his voice and pointing a few feet away from the circle. "At least until I'm done."

He kept grumbling under his breath as we walked away.

"Sumerians? Really?"

"It's a theory, and one with strong evidence to support it," Monty said, looking down at the circle. "This circle is a masterclass in teleportation."

"Really?" I said, looking down at it. "It looks like any other teleportation circle to me. Why is it special?"

"An interplanar teleportation circle with a subtle cast built in to mask our arrival," Monty said, pointing at certain areas as he described it. "How is that even possible? The circle alone should be impossible."

"It is," Dex said with a wicked grin, "for anyone who isn't me."

"Incredible," Monty said, awed as he looked down at the slowly turning violet circle. "This skill is astounding."

Dex waved Monty's words away.

"Focus up, the both of you, and step in," Dex said, motioning for us to get in the circle now. "When you get there, you should be in the middle of the Simum Market. You're looking for Anu. Don't dally. He's tall, dark skinned, well-built"—he snapped his fingers as if trying to remember —"looks like that British chap, the actor all the ladies melt over. Very popular fellow. What's his name... Ris, Reese, Melba."

"Idris Elba?" I hazarded a guess. "The actor?"

"That's it!" Dex said, pointing at me. "He looks like an older version of this Idris fellow. You speak only to him, and you tell him you may have a shadewalker problem. You tell him I sent you, but he'll know that part once he sees these."

Dex gestured and three green symbols descended from his fingers: one falling on Monty, one on me, and one on Peaches.

"A shadewalker," Monty said. "Are you certain?"

"It's the only thing that makes sense," Dex answered, patting Peaches on the head and forming three large sausages on the ground in front of him. "Those are for the trip."

Peaches proceeded to inhale one of the sausages as Dex chuckled.

"What's a shadewalker?" I asked, removing the other two sausages from impending inhalation by hellhound and putting them away in my jacket pocket. "How bad is it?"

"If you break this curse, not too bad."

"And if we don't?"

"Well, considering Taylor was a deathcaster, if he manages to return fully, Tristan will become undead."

"Undead?"

"And a slave to Taylor."

"What the... are you serious?"

"And you will give him an infinite supply of life energy, being immortal and all that," Dex said. "I'd say that would be pretty bad. But don't despair! Anu is an expert in these things —if he's still alive that is—and he'll have a solution."

I stared at Dex who was incredibly calm as he described this worst-case scenario.

"I'm not feeling the confidence here, Dex," I said. "You're not even sure if this Anu person is alive?"

"I'm fairly certain he's alive," Dex said, nudging me all the way into the circle. "At least sixty, sixty-five percent certain. He's bloody hard to kill—I should know, I've tried at least five times, or was it six? I've lost track."

"Sixty-five percent?" I asked. "We're supposed to go do this based on a sixty-five percent chance?"

"I've risked more on less," Dex assured me. "You'll be fine. This circle will bypass your plane to Anu's plane. If he is there, he will help you. Just mention my name and let him see the symbols. Tristan, you can reveal them if needed, yes?"

"Yes," Monty said with a nod.

"Do we even know why Taylor is after Monty?"

"I never said Taylor is after my nephew," Dex said. "He will want you. Somehow you, your blade, and that whole situation with Lotus stabbing Keeper Gault, opened the door. He has no need for Tristan, except as a minion. He *will* want you and your blade, though. Weren't you paying attention?"

"I was and I am," I said, thrown by the turn of events. "How do we stop him? Wait—why my blade?"

Dex glared at me and then turned to Monty.

"Explain it to him, please," Dex said with a sigh. "When you arrive, try not to draw too much attention to yourselves. Find Anu and break this curse. If I'm right about this, Taylor is tethered to one or both of you because of the blade. Whatever you do, do not let Taylor get his hands on Ebonsoul. That would be bad."

He stepped out of the circle and placed a hand on the

edge, touching several symbols in the process. The circle began rotating faster and faster until the symbols were a blur. With a violet flash, Dex and the school of battle magic were gone.

SIXTEEN

We arrived in the center of a desert.

The hot sun blazed down on us as I looked around. Everywhere I looked it was dunes of sand. They went on as far as the eye could see, making an ocean of rust-colored sand extending into the horizon in every direction.

"This doesn't appear to be the Simum Market," Monty said. "Or *any* market at all, for that matter."

"What makes you say that?" I asked. "The fact that everywhere we look it's just sand?"

"Well, yes," Monty said, looking up at the blazing sun. "Where *did* my uncle teleport us?"

"He teleported us into the Sahara," I said, wiping my brow as the sun baked my head. "This is just perfect. Where are we? Do you have any idea? Are your mage senses giving you any clues?"

Monty looked around, raising a hand to shade his eyes as he turned in a slow circle. After about ten seconds of a slow rotation, peering into the distance, he faced me again.

"I have no bloody idea," he said. "This is not our plane, or any plane I recognize. It would appear my uncle made a slight miscalculation."

I stared at him.

"A slight miscalculation?" I asked. "This is a *slight miscalculation?*"

"I just said that," Monty said, peering off into the distance again. "This place does seem quite barren."

"You needed to turn in a dramatic circle to tell me what I already knew?" I said, raising my voice. "Why would Dex teleport us to Tatooine?"

"This is Kengir, not Tatooine."

"How do you even know?" I asked, my voice slightly tinged with panic. "You've never been to Kengir."

"My apologies. I hadn't realized how familiar you were with desert planets," he said without looking in my direction. "Can you refresh my memory? How many trips have been made to Tatooine?"

"Not even slightly funny," I said with a growl. "Do you sense any energy signatures? Anything or anyone? Are we the only living beings in this desert?"

"Unlikely."

Peaches let out a low rumble and growled. He nudged my leg, managing to swipe one of the sausages from my hand while I was distracted, and inhaling it before I could react.

<Hey! No eating the sausages!>

<The old man said they were for the trip. We are on the trip.>

<This is not a trip. This is a nightmare.>

<Sweet men are coming.>

<Sweet men? What does that mean?>

<They smell sweet. They are coming here.>

Off in the distance, I saw a plume of dust rising into the air. The shimmering heat distorted the image, but it appeared to be men on horseback.

"We have company," I said, making sure I had easy access to Grim Whisper. "Can you sense their energy signatures?"

Monty closed his eyes and focused for a few seconds, before shaking his head.

"I can't tell," he said. "This plane...my access to my ability is different on this plane, limited somehow. I can tell they wield energy, but not much more than that. We need to tread carefully."

"I can't sense anything either, but it seems Peaches can read them," I said, patting my hellhound's ginormous head. "Called them sweet."

"Sweet?" Monty said, looking at the figures in the distance. "Why sweet?"

"How exactly would I know how to explain that?" I said. "Do I look like the hellhound whisperer? Looks like three of them."

"Let's treat them as civil until proven otherwise," Monty said, dusting off his sleeves as the men approached. "No need to start things off on the wrong foot."

"Civil until proven otherwise works," I said, looking up into the brutal sun again. "I hope they have water. Peaches isn't going to last long in this heat."

"Pardon me?" Monty said, turning to me with a look of disbelief. "He isn't going to last long in the *what*?"

"This is a desert, Monty," I explained slowly, waving an arm around. "Have you not noticed your uncle dumped us on Arrakis? Prolonged heat is bad for canines. They overheat."

"I'm beginning to think the heat is detrimentally affecting your faculties. Are you feeling ill?"

"We haven't been here long enough for the heat to bother me," I said, wiping the sweat from my brow. "Why do you ask?"

"Simon...he is a *hellhound*," Monty clarified. "I don't think the *heat* is going to be an issue for your creature. It's right there in the name…*hell*hound?"

"You don't know that," I said, rubbing my hellhound's head. "He's still a puppy. The heat could be bad for him."

"Actually, I'm fairly certain heat will never be an issue for him, judging from the lakes of lava his father was casually protecting during our visit to Hades."

Peaches kept his gaze on the riders getting closer.

<Are you too hot, boy?>

<I'm never too hot. But you are looking red, bondmate. Are you too hot?>

I removed my jacket and held it over my head to provide some shade.

<I'll be ok. Can you smell if these people are good or bad?>

<They don't smell bad. They smell different. Sweet.>

<Sweet? Since when do people smell sweet?>

<Since I smelled these people coming. I hope they have meat. The meat the old man made me is gone.>

The last sausage was gone. I looked around, marveling at his meat inhalation skills.

<Because you ate it?>

<I was supposed to eat it. He said it was for the trip. We are on the trip. I ate it.>

As the riders drew closer, I was able to confirm more definitively that there were three of them in total. Two of the riders hung back, but one kept approaching. I couldn't accurately gauge their distance. It had to be the heat shimmer, the effect of the heat on the sand messing with my vision.

The black horses they were riding made Clydesdales appear like toy ponies. Seeing their true size as the rider got closer, I realized these horses were easily twice the size of the largest Clydesdale I had ever seen.

All three men were dressed in nomadic clothing, reminding me of desert-dwelling Bedouin tribes. They all wore white and light brown robes, with a long gown over a pair of trousers. Around their waists I saw thick belts, and over their shoulders, long cloaks.

Around their heads they had wrapped a similarly light-brown material, which was held in place with darker strips of material. The rider in the center, probably the leader, wore a deep-orange turban with some symbols I couldn't understand along the front.

Strapped to their sides, for easy access, I noticed the large, curved knives covered in softly glowing, orange runes—and on the left side of each of the robes, I saw the symbol of a blazing sun in a deep red.

SEVENTEEN

I took another step back as the riders approached.

"I know we may be strangers here," I said, keeping my voice low, "but I recognize a badge when I see one. Sun Council?"

"It would seem so," Monty said, keeping his face impassive and his voice just as low. "My question is, how did they know we were here, and what brought them to us with such urgency? We are, apparently, in the middle of nowhere, and yet they knew to come directly to us. That does not bode well."

"Diplomacy?"

He nodded.

"Civil until proven otherwise."

The lead rider came forward and settled his mount, who snorted as they got close. It probably had something to do with the low growls and smiles Peaches was sharing with our new friends.

<Don't attack them…at least, not yet, boy.>

<If they don't attack, I won't. Their big animals are not friendly.>

He was right.

I could tell from the stamping and snorting that their oversized horses looked ready to trample us into the sand. The lead rider was having some difficulty keeping his horse creature under control, and the two in the rear looked skittish and angry.

I wondered if these were warhorses, bred for battle, or if they were just native to the desert and preferred to be running wild, rather than serving as mounts for the Sun Council.

I stared openly at the horses, because my brain was having trouble processing them. I had never seen anything like them. They were fearsomely beautiful, with a clear intelligence in their eyes.

Each of the horses carried water skins and large packs attached to one side, and I saw the hilts of swords peeking out of sheaths attached to the other side of the oversized animals.

The lead horse stared at me, not with aggression, but with a sort of amused curiosity. The other two in the rear were just having a bad day and wanted out. Their riders backed off a little more and the horses calmed down—it seemed to be a proximity thing.

"Strangers," the lead rider called out, touching his heart and then touching his forehead while he was still some distance away, "Welcome to Kengir. How may we assist you?"

"Thank you for this kind welcome," Monty said, repeating the heart-and-head gesture. "We seem to be somewhat off course."

Monty looked around before glancing up at the lead rider.

The man followed Monty's gaze, looked at us oddly for a few seconds, and then smiled.

That smile kicked off all the alarms in my head.

It was the kind of smile someone gave you right before they buried a blade in your chest.

These men weren't friendly. Suddenly, I wasn't feeling very welcome. It was the same feeling I got when I wandered into the wrong neighborhood at the wrong time, all while dressed the wrong way.

"I'm getting a major Hotel California vibe from this patrol," I muttered under my breath. "Their lips say welcome, but their body language says we're not exactly *guests* of the Sun Council."

"We play it by ear," Monty said, keeping his voice just as low. "So far they haven't drawn their weapons."

"The day is young," I said, pointing forward with my chin. "Heads up—he's coming closer."

The lead rider closed the distance and brought his giant horse even closer to us. It was even more impressive up close, standing around ten feet at the shoulder, with a glistening black coat which shone in the sun.

"As I mentioned earlier, we are somewhat lost," Monty said. "Perhaps you can assist us?"

"Of course. You are travelers of light, and you are in the land of Kengir," the man said. "Where exactly would you like to go?"

"Simum Market," Monty said, glancing to the side. "Perhaps you can orient and point us in the right direction. We would greatly appreciate it, and would be in your debt."

"I can do better than that," the lead rider said, placing a hand on his chest. "I am Kish; to my left is Larsa, and the other is Ruppak." Both men touched their hearts and heads at the mention of their names. "You must allow me and my companions the honor of escorting you to Simum. You are two days travel from the market by sandsteed." He patted the large horse's neck which snorted at the touch. "Walking there is out of the question. There are many dangers, and you would not survive this trip. I would hate to have evil befall you while visiting my home. Where are you from?"

Unless it has already befallen us by meeting you.

The last question was almost a throwaway. He said it so nonchalantly, it was designed to be answered almost as a reflex.

Monty and I remained silent—because he knew better than to answer the sand police and me? Because I didn't have the information he wanted.

I didn't even know how to begin to answer the question. What did we say? Earth 616? Did the planes have special designations, and if they did, what were they? I certainly didn't know them. I wasn't that frequent a plane traveler; I barely left New York City, much less the plane I lived in.

"Some distance abroad," Monty said with the same nonchalance, answering without really answering. "I would hate to trouble you and impose on your companions. We only need the direction. We can manage to get there on our own."

"Out of the question," Kish replied, shaking his head. "You are not dressed for the sands or the sun, and we carry no spare clothing. I must insist that you come with us."

"I feel we are only causing you trouble," Monty said, holding up a hand in surrender. "You must be in the midst of some important duties, being out here alone in the middle of nowhere."

"It is no trouble, really," Kish replied with another smile. "I will not take no for an answer. The rules of hospitality make your safety my obligation. You are a guest in my land. I know you are not familiar with our ways, but I would consider it an insult—not only to me, but to our clan—to leave you here alone to fend for yourselves. There are thieves and worse roaming these sands."

I bet.

"One moment," Monty said, raising a hand as he stepped closer to me. "Allow me a word to speak to my companion."

"Please, please," Kish said, motioning to Monty to speak to me, before looking to his companions, who nodded to him. "However, do not delay too long. These sands are not safe for the natural-born dwellers of Kengir, much less for those who visit them from *some distance abroad*. Do not tarry. We cannot be on the sand after dark if we value our lives."

Monty stepped close to me and turned his back to the riders. Peaches remained facing Kish and his companions while giving them his best hellhound smile.

It was probably the reason they didn't get any closer.

"Your thoughts?" Monty asked, keeping his voice low. "They don't intend to leave us alone. That much is clear."

"A two-day ride, if they're telling the truth, on those sand-steeds sounds like quite a distance," I said. "Gauging how fast they got here, and the approximate distance they covered from the moment we spotted them, to the moment they got here...hard to do without any landmarks, true, but they can cover distance, quick." I peeked over Monty's shoulder. "And these sandsteeds don't seem tired or bothered by this heat. We wouldn't make it too far on foot. No way we can outrun them."

"Especially since we don't know which direction to head in," he added. "The ambient energy of this plane was a definite factor in my uncle's miscalculation."

"Can you use your wiggle-fingers here?" I asked. "We have our blades, but those daggers look enhanced."

"I noticed the runes," he said. "If we were alone, I could conduct some tests to see the extent of my ability on this plane. I'm hesitant to do so with an audience. I could be revealing potential weaknesses."

"True," I said, glancing at Kish and his friends. "They

don't seem the least bothered by Peaches. Don't you find that weird?"

"I do find the lack of a reaction worrisome," he said. "Hellhounds are not considered a naturally occurring part of the fauna on most planes."

I nodded.

"Most people who encounter my amazing hellhound can't help but remark in some way, good or bad," I said, patting my hellhound along the sides. "But not indifferent. No one remains neutral. That seems off."

"It only makes sense in the worst-case scenario," Monty said. "This is a termination team."

I nodded.

"They've already written us off and we're just going through the formalities now," I said. "I've seen that. Don't attach, don't engage more than you have to. Keep the interaction to one member of the team."

"Also indicative of how they've spaced themselves out," Monty said. "Gives the other two the time and space to react in case something goes wrong or we're overtly hostile."

"Makes me wonder about their power level, though," I said. "Why not dust us and keep moving?"

"Too many variables," Monty said. "They don't know our power levels or what your creature can or can't do. Better to do this methodically. Eliminate the element of surprise."

"True. Walk us out a few miles in this desert, get us tired, thirsty, and slow, then end us. No one is going to find us out here."

"I doubt anyone is looking," Monty said. "For now, we have to play their game."

"Going on the record as saying this game sucks."

"Duly noted. If they do intend to hasten our demise, there will be some excuse as to why they can't offer us one of these sandsteeds," Monty said, glancing over his shoulder. "If their real concern is getting us quickly to Simum Market, one of the three will offer us a mount, and double up with a companion in the spirit of hospitality and expediency."

"So, if we're walking they intend to make this the last walk we ever take," I said with a short nod. "Should we try and find out more about what the Sun Council is, or should we wait until they reveal the intention to bury us out here, first?"

"I thought I was the cynic," Monty said, his back still turned to Kish. "Let's find out which it is first, and then we can ask about this Sun Council. I'm sure it's a benevolent group of desert nomads whose only concern is rescuing the lost wanderers of the sands."

"Like us?"

"Exactly like us: travelers of the light."

"I call BS," I muttered mostly to myself. "Let them know."

Monty turned and touched his heart and head again as he smiled.

"We have chosen to accept your kind offer of guidance and hospitality," Monty said. "We are honored to have your company as you escort us to Simum Market."

Kish slowly moved his hand from his belt, which was surprisingly close to the blade on his waist, and gave us a wide smile.

"That is a very good choice my friends," he said. "Unfortunately, as you can see, we do not have a spare sandsteed. You will have to walk until we join our larger caravan, which is a half a day's journey away from here."

"That is not very far," Monty said. "Would you be able to provide water for our support dog? He gets very thirsty."

Kish's expression turned ugly, but he quickly recovered.

"We would not waste—My apologies... We cannot spare water for your creature," Kish said. "We have very specific rations. If we misuse them, we place our sandsteeds at risk.

There will be much to drink at the gathering of our caravan. There is a well there. Do not worry."

"Your caravan is headed to Simum?" I asked, glancing up into the sun. "Half a day away?"

"Yes," Kish answered as he turned his steed around. "We are all headed to Simum Market. We will resupply and provide you both with sandsteeds when we meet up with our larger group."

"Deathmarch it is," I said under my breath. "Half a day until they try to end us. Always nice to know when it's coming, at least."

"Clarity provides decisive action," Monty said as we started walking forward. "Keep your wits about you."

"Always."

Kish headed out in front of us, while Larsa and Ruppak brought up the rear, keeping the same triangular formation. Monty, Peaches, and me were sandwiched between them.

The sun blazed and baked us as we walked.

EIGHTEEN

We had been walking for close to ten minutes when I sensed a shift in the energy around us.

The two riders behind us became agitated and spoke to Kish in a language I didn't understand. They motioned with their arms and pointed off into the distance behind us several times.

"You catch that?" I asked. "Seems something has them worried."

"If by 'catch that', you mean, 'Did I fail to understand any of it,' then yes, I caught it," Monty said glancing behind us. "I did feel the shift in energy. It made them nervous."

"Nervous enough to switch languages," I said with a small smile. "Whatever they sensed, has them spooked. Maybe we can offer our services?"

"Or at the very least unnerve them," Monty said. "Worth a try. Time to play the difficult hostage."

Monty cleared his throat, raised a hand, and removed a shoe, pouring sand out of it as he stopped. His actions caused us all to stop.

"Deepest apologies, my friends," he said, pointing to his

shoes. "These are not designed for desert travel." He raised a sleeve to his forehead to wipe away the sweat. "Bloody hell, it is hot, isn't it?"

"It is the desert," Larsa—at least I think it was Larsa—said, dryly and with a major dose of contempt. "It is always hot. We must keep walking."

"In a moment," Monty said, laying it on thick. "My feet are *absolutely* killing me. Do you think we can take a moment to sit? Perhaps we could string up a few of your robes and construct a makeshift camp? That would be capital."

Kish stared at Monty with thinly veiled surprise and anger.

"You want us to remove *our* robes to provide you and your companion with shade?" Kish asked as he turned around. "Is that what you are requesting?"

"Don't forget our support canine," Monty added, pointing at Peaches. "He does get very hot. Are you sure you don't have some water to spare for him? I would greatly appreciate it."

I thought Kish was going to burst a blood vessel as he shook his head no. He didn't seem happy about the makeshift camp suggestion. It may have had something to do with the entitled attitude Monty used when he made his request.

"We cannot stop," Larsa said, probably because the power of coherent speech had escaped Kish. "Do not make foolish requests."

"It's only for a short time," Monty said. "At least until my companion and I cool off a bit. This heat is quite brutal. Would it be possible to make camp at least until the sun drops a bit? We are quite exhausted and, unlike you, we lack sandsteeds."

"You are tired?" Kish asked. "We have only been walking for a short time." He said something in his native language and all three riders laughed as they glanced at us. I couldn't understand the words, but I certainly understood the tone. It was probably something along the lines of us being soft, and not cut out for the harsh life of the desert. "We still have much sand to cross."

"We just need to sit for a short time," Monty said, picking the sand out of his shoes with an exasperated huff. "In the meantime, we can all cool off. You three must be quite warm and your steeds—"

"Out of the question," Kish said, cutting him off and glancing behind us. "We must keep moving."

I did my best to hide the smile at Monty's performance. He had missed his calling becoming a mage—, he should have focused on drama and acting instead. He played the difficult hostage to perfection.

"Why?" I asked, looking behind us. "There's no one else out here except us. Why are we rushing? We should wait. Won't your caravan wait for you? They *will* wait for you, won't they?"

Monty gave me a slight nod and proceeded to dump more sand from his other shoe. At this point, I was wondering where all the sand was coming from. Was he creating more sand without them noticing?

"My companion has a point," Monty said shaking out the sand. "Are we in a dire need for urgency? If we slow down—"

"No," Kish said abruptly. "We must not slow down. We have lost enough time as it is."

"I don't think they're being entirely honest, Monty," I said, raising my voice. "I think our good friend Kish here is keeping something from us. What do you think?"

"I think,"—Monty held up his shoe and turned it around, examining it—"my shoes are completely ruined. Do you realize these are Armani?"

"They are?" I said playing into my role. "I had no idea. Are you sure they're ruined?"

"Armani does not make desert footwear," Monty said with a huff. "They are not designed for sand." He held up his shoe again. "My shoes are ruined. We need to slow down or stop."

"We cannot slow down or stop," Kish said, exasperated. "We must go...now."

"I need a moment," Monty said. "My shoes are dead."

I nearly burst out with laughter, but managed to keep a straight face as I considered that the sand police were probably rushing us to our death.

"I don't see why we can't wait a short time," I said, glancing behind us again as Larsa looked nervously over his shoulder. "We'll get there eventually, right?"

I had placed them in an impossible position. If they kept trying to rush us, they would have to explain why. If they admitted that their caravan would wait, they would have to be okay with us sitting for a while.

Either way, they were either stuck or else would have to fabricate some monster to keep us moving. I waited for Kish to answer.

Kish seemed to have picked up on my strategy. Sitting back on his steed for a moment, he gathered himself before spreading his arms wide, sharing another one of his brilliant smiles.

This was definitely a I can't wait to stab you in the neck with my dagger smile.

"My dear friends, I am sorry you are *tired*. We cannot 'make camp' as you request," Kish said. "There are many enemies in these lands. Strangers such as yourself are in grave danger."

"From whom?" Monty asked, looking around. "There is no one else here we can see."

"Exactly! There are enemies you cannot see, who use their abilities to hide themselves from simple sight," Kish explained. "You are unskilled and cannot see or sense them.

You are not from the sand, but we have roamed the sand since before we could walk. We are sensitive to these enemies."

"These enemies," I said. "They're people like you? They have that sun picture on their robes?"

He looked down at the image of the sun on his chest, then looked at me with narrowed eyes.

"Like us? No," Kish said, glancing behind us again. "They are less than my people. They are filth, creatures of the sand, and given to killing and devouring the strangers unfortunate enough to become lost among the sacred sand."

Sacred sand definitely raised a few alarms in my head. I glanced at Monty, who picked up my look and gave me a subtle nod. In my experience, when inanimate objects took on divine status, I was dealing with some kind of zealot.

Last time I checked, sand wasn't sacred, no matter what plane I was on, but I kept my opinion to myself.

"Sand cannibals?" I asked, incredulously looking from side to side. "You're telling us there's sand cannibals out here? Monsters that eat people? Strangers like us?"

I added a bit extra panic to my voice, and hoped I didn't go over the top.

"Sand cannibals?" Monty echoed. "I dare say we can't sit around and wait for them to devour us. We must leave with all haste! Thank you, my dear friends for extricating us from this predicament."

He quickly put on his shoes and starting walking. Kish shot his companions a look that said, *Can you believe how gullible these two are?*

We started walking again, at a faster pace this time.

"Thank you," I repeated as Kish led the way. "We would've been in serious trouble if you hadn't found us. By the way, how exactly did you find us? We're in the middle of nowhere."

Larsa and Ruppak glanced at each other, but said nothing, keeping their faces impassive.

"An excellent question," Monty said, staring at Kish. "How did you find us? Of course, I want you to know that we are eternally grateful—not to mention fortunate!—that you found us, despite the fact that my feet are killing me. Still, you saved us from a fate worse than death. How *did* you do it?"

There was another shift in energy behind us and this one caused them to speak in their native tongue among themselves in a rapid-fire sequence. It seemed Larsa and Ruppak wanted to cut their losses, but Kish felt we still held value... until Larsa looked back and called out something to Kish, who stopped.

I turned and in the distance, saw a solitary figure walking along the sand, heading our way. Both Larsa and Ruppak were agitated now, pointing at us and then pointing at the figure in the distance. I managed to pick up one word over and over, especially when they pointed at the figure behind us.

The word they kept repeating was *ush*.

NINETEEN

"What does *ush* mean?" I asked. "Your men keep saying it and pointing at that man. Do you know him? Is he a friend of yours? Should we wait for him?"

"No!" Larsa and Ruppak said simultaneously. "He is *ush*!"

"Ush?" I said to Kish. "Is that his name,? Ush? Are we going to wait for Ush?"

Ruppak paled as he backed away from the approaching man.

"It is not important," Kish said, lowering his voice as he waved my words away. "Be silent. We are in danger."

"Danger?" Monty said, serious now. "Do you need assistance?"

"From you?" Kish asked incredulously. "Do not be a fool! I would sooner ask a sandsteed to speak than a stranger like you for help against that thing."

"That *thing*?" Monty said, gazing behind us. "It looks like a man. Are you saying it's not a man?"

Kish ignored him and had more words with his companions. After a few minutes, Kish and Larsa dismounted, but

Ruppak remained on his sandsteed. The heated conversation continued, and then Ruppak took off at a full gallop.

"Where is he going?" I asked, looking after Ruppak and then turning slowly to peer at the figure behind us, which was much closer now. "There's only one man. Is he afraid of one man?"

"He is getting help," Kish said, reaching into the bags that were strapped to the sides of the sandsteeds, and pulling out short swords, which resembled their daggers, but on a larger scale. "If we are still alive when he returns he will help us. If we are dead, he will avenge us."

"It's only one man," I said again, still looking at the figure. "We need help for one man?"

"For this one man, yes," Kish said, turning to us. "This is no ordinary man."

I peered into the distance at the man approaching us.

"Looks pretty ordinary to me," I said. "What's so special about him? You and your companion seem pretty nervous."

"Silence!" Kish demanded. "Or I will slit your throats where you stand and be rid of you."

I backed up and raised both hands in surrender.

"No need to get hostile," I said. "You could have just asked for quiet."

Kish glared daggers at me.

Monty peered after Ruppak for a few seconds, and then turned to gaze at the mysterious man approaching us.

"Why is he here?" Monty asked, turning to Kish. "What called him?"

Kish said some words to Larsa, who produced a sword similar to Kish's. Larsa moved faster than my eye could track and ended up behind Monty, holding the sword against his neck.

"What are you doing?" I said, raising my voice. "Let him go. This is how you treat guests in your land?"

"This is how we treat the deathtouched in our land, yes," Kish spat. "We are going to offer your blood to the sand. The deathtouched are cursed and only deserve one thing—death."

"Deathtouched?" I asked. "What does that even mean?"

Larsa held the blade tight against Monty's neck. Any sudden movement would cause him to slit Monty's neck with ease.

"You have both been cursed, touched by *ush*," Larsa said. "Death has touched you."

"Ush appears to mean death in their native tongue," Monty said. "They seem to frown upon it."

"We are not deathtouched, whatever that means," I protested. "Let him go, and we'll leave you alone."

"You don't understand," Kish said as the man kept approaching. "We are the Sun Council. It is our duty to eliminate the deathtouched. Even if we let you go, we must remove you from our land. We must spill your blood to bring back the balance."

Not the sand police—they were a death patrol. Fantastic.

"How about you just let us go back where we came from?" I asked, slowly trying to get closer to Larsa and Monty. "If we just left your desert, would that restore the balance?"

"Your feet have touched the sacred sands," Kish said. "A price must be exacted...a price in blood."

"Why does it always have to be blood?" I asked mostly to myself. "Maybe we can come to an understanding. Our feet didn't really touch the sacred sands. It was more our shoes."

"His feet touched our land," Kish said, pointing at Monty with his sword. "He has defiled our land and must pour out his blood. And you...you reek of death. You both deserve to be buried in the sacred sands."

"That was the plan all along, wasn't it?" I asked. "From the moment we got here, you were prepared to end us, weren't you?"

"We have an old saying among my people: nothing good comes unbidden from the sacred sands," Kish answered. "Yes. The moment we knew what you were, we were making preparations to offer your bodies to the sacred sands."

"Offer our bodies to the sacred sands," I said mostly to myself. "You weren't going to take us to Simum Market?"

"To contaminate our people and our homes? Are you mad?"

"Just checking," I said. "I knew that whole sacred sands thing was going to be an issue."

"The sacred sands must not be defiled," Kish snapped. "You have brought death to our lands."

"Only one I see holding a blade to my friend's neck is your companion," I said. "Let him go."

"We cannot," Kish said. "His blood must feed the sand."

I really, truly hated dealing with zealots. I took a deep breath and let it out slowly. One last chance to try diplomacy. I made a mental note to inform Dex that his interplanar teleportation skills needed major work.

"What do you plan on doing?" I asked, keeping my voice even. "I can promise you that before his body drops to the ground, you and your man will be dead."

Kish laughed.

"You are no warrior," he said. "You are weak and can barely withstand the sun. I am Kengir and live the light and sand. My bones were formed walking the sands as a child. You are soft. You and your friend will die here today. This is truth."

The stranger had gotten close, but not too close. He wore clothing similar to Kish and Larsa, but his face was mostly covered, leaving only his copper-colored eyes visible.

This man possessed a powerful energy signature and carried a long rune-covered staff of rich, deep mahogany. He stopped some distance away and stared at Kish, before gazing at Larsa.

"Hold, Kish," the man said, his deep voice resounding across the desert. "These men have no quarrel with you. They are here for me."

"All the more reason to end their lives, Anu," Kish said. "You are trafficking in the deathtouched now? Have you no shame?"

"Do not do this, brother," Anu said, holding his arms out to his sides. "We are one people. There is no need to spill blood."

"I am not your brother! They are not my people!" Kish snarled. "They are deathtouched! That one"—he pointed at me—"is fouled by death and has brought it here...here! To the sacred sands! They violated the law, and must be punished!"

Anu shook his head slowly.

"He did not know. They did not know," Anu said, looking at Monty and me. "I plead mercy for their case. They are ignorant of our ways and customs."

"You know that is no excuse," Kish said. "Ignorance of the law is no defense. You were Sun Council once, long ago. Have you forgotten the sacred tenets?"

"I have not," Anu said. "But these men are here as my guests. Is this what defines our hospitality now?"

"You offer hospitality to the cursed?" Kish scoffed. "You are no better than this creature of hell"—he pointed at Peaches—"and deserve to die just as equally."

I opened my eyes in surprise as he mentioned Peaches.

"Yes," Kish said with a satisfied nod. "I was aware of your helldog the moment it set foot on my land. You wanted to know how we found you? You hold a necrotic blade, your animal belongs to the depths of hell, and your companion has been touched by darkness and death. The stench of your evil fills my land. The all-powerful sacred sand cries out for justice and balance. We are trained to sense such things."

"The sand, or your leaders, who have twisted the teachings of our people?" Anu asked, cupping an ear and listening to the silence. "If the all-powerful sands require justice and balance, let it act. Let it exact justice and balance."

"Blasphemer," Kish hissed. "The Sun Council are the hands and feet of the sacred sands. We act for them and speak the unutterable. It has always been this way and it will always be so."

<Boy, the moment he tries to hurt Monty, you stop him>

<Can I bite him?>

<Yes, but be careful. He may smell sweet, but these people are rotten and confused to the core. You don't want that in your stomach. It will probably poison you. Treat him like Monty's shoes—chew, but don't swallow.>

<Chew, but don't swallow. Can I chew on the both of them?>

<Right now, just focus on the one with the blade to Monty's neck. Later, if we have time, you can mangle his friend too.>

<I'm ready.>

"Convenient, is what it is," Anu said calmly. "Especially against one who cannot defend himself. Stop this now, Kish, and you will leave in peace."

"I have summoned a full circle of sandsteeds," Kish said. "We will deal with you once and for all, Anu."

"A full circle," Anu said, peering off into the distance. "You humble me. I do not merit a full circle; perhaps half, but not a full circle. Prefect Bau must be quite upset. Does he still hold me responsible for the destruction of the temple?"

"You *were* responsible for the temple's destruction!" Kish yelled. "You destroyed the cornerstone that weakened the entire structure, then unleashed a blast that toppled the temple!"

"No one died," Anu answered. "All of the Sun Council clerics were saved. Only the building was destroyed."

"A building that took a sixth of a circle to build and complete," Kish said. "Bau is looking forward to your prolonged torture and death, heretic."

"It warms my heart to know that I am still in Bau's thoughts," Anu said. "The atrocities committed in the name of the sand needed to be stopped. I merely chose the optimal target."

"You will bleed for your heresy," Kish said. "I will see your blood run in the sacred sand."

"Not today," Anu said, glancing upward to the sun. "The sacred sands will be denied blood today—unless you wish to spill your own?"

"You dare blaspheme?" Kish said raising his voice. "You speak against the sacred sands?"

"I dare. I cannot allow you to harm these men," Anu said. "They come to me from a dear friend and, as such, I must extend hospitality to them—true hospitality, not this farce you pretend to display."

"You choose them over your own people?"

"I do," Anu said. "Especially when my own people have betrayed the true teachings."

"Very well. You can die with them," Kish said and nodded to Larsa. "Start with that one."

<Now, boy!>

Peaches blinked out of sight.

TWENTY

Peaches reappeared half a second later and clamped onto Larsa's arm, pulling the blade away from Monty's neck.

Monty drove an elbow into Larsa's face and rolled away from the blade. Peaches blinked out, taking Larsa with him.

Kish whirled on me, sword drawn and aimed at me.

"Where is my companion?" Kish demanded. "Tell your helldog to bring him back now!"

"I don't know where he went," I shot back with a shrug as I backed up. "But wherever he took him, I hope he loses him there."

"You are not on your plane," Kish said and raised a hand. "The rules are different here, as you are about to discover."

He made a gesture, formed a fist, and made another gesture with his fingers splayed out. A bright blue flash blinded me as Peaches and Larsa spilled out onto the sand and rolled away.

Peaches managed to stand and then wobbled over onto his side.

"What did you do?" I said as I ran over to his side. "What did you do to him?"

"Bau will want him for study," Kish said. "I merely slowed him down to make him manageable. He will be studied, and then disposed of."

"Disposed of? You're going to have to kill me first," I said my voice low and menacing. "You will *not* touch my hellhound."

"Oh?" Kish said. "Haven't you been paying attention? None of you are leaving the sands *alive*. A full circle—my apologies, your number system is crude and primitive—three hundred and sixty sandsteeds, with some of the fiercest Sun Council warriors, are on their way here as we speak. Where can you run? You cannot escape. It's over."

"You always were so full of yourself, Kish," Anu said. "A full circle won't be enough. Even if Bau sent two full circles, it wouldn't be enough."

"Empty boasting," Kish said and closed on Anu. "I have been wanting to silence you since the destruction of the temple."

"Why wait?" Anu said. "I stand here now. This is your opportunity. Take it—or do you fear me?"

"Fear you?" Kish seethed. "I am superior to you in every way. I have not betrayed our ways. I have remained true. You....you have become anathema, a curse to be despised and destroyed."

"Then do it," Anu said, moving away from us into an open area. "If I am to be despised and destroyed, here I stand. Destroy me... if you can."

"I can and shall," Kish said, aiming his sword and rushing at Anu. "Today you die by my hand."

Kish lunged forward and slashed with his blade. Anu deflected the slash with his staff and slashed downward, sending up a small column of sand into Kish's face, blinding him.

"Tricks and deceptions," Kish said, slashing through the

column of sand and destroying it. "You fight as cowards do, hiding behind illusion and misdirection."

"Not as cowards do," Anu said, sidestepping a lunge and evading a slash while striking back with his staff. "As those who are outnumbered do."

Larsa joined the fight and attacked from the rear. Anu spun, slamming his staff into Larsa's head and sending him flying off to the side.

"Not very sporting, attacking from the rear, don't you think?" Anu asked as Kish slid forward and slashed at his legs, forcing Anu to jump back to avoid the attack. "Is that what is being taught in the Sun Council these days? Rear attacks?"

Anu landed some distance away and glanced at Monty and me, before looking down at Peaches.

"Can he move?" Anu asked me. "He may need to run very soon."

"No one is running anywhere," Kish said with a laugh. "Listen...listen to your approaching death."

A low rumble filled the air.

Monty ran over to my fallen hellhound and placed his hands on his side. He said some words under his breath and his hands began to glow gold.

Kish and Larsa beat their swords along the sand and screamed.

"He defiles the sacred sand!" Kish yelled. "He must die!"

Peaches jumped to his feet and growled.

"Stop him," Anu said, pointing behind Kish and Larsa. "We are running out of time!"

I looked into the distance and saw a black cloud on the horizon.

Anu closed on Kish and Larsa.

"We can't have you following us," Anu said, smashing one end of his staff into Kish's knee, breaking it, while he drove the tips of his fingers across Larsa's eyes, temporarily blinding him. "That should hold you still. Be grateful I don't have more time to correct you."

He turned to Monty and me. "You two, with me. That group won't be as reasonable as these two."

He took off running and we took off after him, the thundering behind us increasing in volume and intensity.

"I don't want to distract you," I said as we ran, "but those sand-horses are gaining on us."

"Over there," Anu said, pointing ahead. "You must make sure to submerge yourself completely, or they will capture you. I cannot save you if you remain behind."

I looked ahead and only saw more sand.

"Submerge ourselves in what? The sand?"

"My apologies," Anu said and slashed the air in front of him. "In that."

An oasis appeared in front of us. Tall palm trees surrounded a small lake of clear blue-green water. Anu traced some gestures as he ran and the surface of the water rippled with blue energy.

"Go!" Anu yelled. "All the way in!"

Behind us, the Sun Council warriors screamed when they saw the oasis. I was getting the distinct feeling they didn't want us to reach the water.

Anu reached the oasis first.

"In you go," he said pushing us to the water. "I will slow them down."

"You can't stay," Monty said. "They will kill you."

"I have no intention of staying. Get in the water."

Monty and I waded into the water until it reached our chests. Peaches was paddling next to me.

"One more thing," Anu said as he peered out at the approaching group. "He really did send a circle. That Bau is an old dog. Time to scatter his fleas."

Anu waved his staff in a circle and pointed at the

approaching Sun Council. A small whirlwind formed in front of him and raced away, picking up speed and growing in size as it rushed at them.

"That should keep them busy," Anu said, dusting off his hands. "Now, in we go."

He jumped in the water and placed a hand on each of our heads. He took a breath, and pushed our heads under the water with enormous strength.

The waters of the oasis of Kengir disappeared.

TWENTY-ONE

We reappeared in the center of a fountain, in the shadow of a tall sculpture of an angel, its wings extended over its waters.

The sun was setting as we waded our way through the water and out onto the plaza the fountain stood within.

Across from the fountain was a two-level terrace made of pink stones, and with that, I immediately recognized where we were. The lower level of the terrace was a large stone plaza, which led to the upper plaza and a pair of majestic stone stairs that led to the street.

We were standing in Bethesda Fountain in the center of Central Park around 72nd Street. The sculpture I had recognized was named Angel in the Waters, and gazed down at us as we stepped out of the fountain. Peaches ran around a few times before stepping completely out of the water.

All of us stepped out of the fountain completely dry— well, all of us except my excited hellhound who felt the fountain made for a perfect hellhound pool.

"It worked," Anu said, looking back at the fountain. "The Park still stands. Excellent."

"You weren't sure it would work?" I said, staring at Anu,

who now held a mahogany walking stick in one hand. He wore a casual black jacket, a cream-colored shirt, dark slacks and a pair of black shoes. "You were unsure?"

"Interplanar travel can be tricky," Anu said, "especially under stress."

I stared because, as Dex had said, I could easily be looking at Idris Elba's older brother.

"Your face," I said, pointing at his face. "That's going to be a problem, even in this city."

"What's wrong with my face?" Anu said raising a hand to his cheek. "Have I become hideous?"

"Quite the contrary," Monty said, looking around to make sure Anu wasn't attracting too much attention. "You look like someone well known."

"This well-known person, is he a criminal?" Anu asked with a smile. "Is he wanted by the authorities? What is he known for? How much devastation has he unleashed?"

"None, unless you count the devastation he's unleashed on women's hearts," I said. "He's not a criminal. He's an actor. We need to leave this plaza."

"An actor?" Anu said. "Do you mean a histrione?"

"A what?" I said confused. "Monty?"

"Yes," Monty said with a nod as he led us out of the plaza. "That is one term for them. You look like a famous histrione."

"He must be quite handsome then," Anu said, glancing at some of the people around the fountain. "Is he very popular?"

"Popular enough that it may become a problem," Monty said. "This way."

Monty led us to the space under the stairs which was part of the lower terrace and also housed seven arches, with three of them forming a tunnel to another set of stairs that led to the upper terrace and the 72nd traverse.

"Hold," Anu said holding out a hand. "We are not alone."

"What?" Monty said. "What do you mean?"

Anu sniffed the air and looked around.

"There are soulless about," Anu said, looking at Monty then me. "Kish was right about one thing: you both have been deathtouched. We must find somewhere safe. Is there holy ground nearby?"

"Holy ground?" I asked. "Like a church?"

"No, not a church," Anu said, looking around. "A place where the dead are buried—a necropolis. There is one to the south, a large one. "

"A necropolis?" I asked. "You want us to find a city of the dead?"

"He means a cemetery or burial ground," Monty said. "How far away do you sense this necropolis?"

"Several miles straight south from where we stand," Anu said, tapping the ground with his walking stick. "We must hurry, or you will find yourself facing soulless without defenses."

"There's no cemetery downtown," I said shaking my head. "Several miles south from where we're standing puts us right in the middle of Tribeca. Do you know how much real estate costs in this city? There's no cemetery in the middle of Tribeca."

"There was," Anu said. "Mage Montague, trust me. We must go with all haste. Take me to this place and I will show you."

"I can't create a circle to a random place," Monty said, shaking his head. "I will get us lost, or worse."

Anu crouched down and placed a hand on the ground.

"This is a place where many have been buried. Thousands," Anu said "Surely this can be no small place."

"Thousands?" I asked. "To find a cemetery that big we'd need to go out to Queens."

"How long ago?" Monty asked. "Can you determine how long ago these people were buried?"

"Monty? Thousands?" I said. "Even if it was one thousand, there is no burial site that large in Tribeca. For thousands, you'd need acres."

Anu was still crouched down with his hand on the ground. I noticed the night was getting darker than usual as the temperature dropped around us. I began seeing my exhaled breaths as the seconds passed.

"Hundreds of years have passed," Anu said. "But their souls linger still."

"Hundreds of years?" Monty said. "South from here?"

"Monty?" I said, concern in my voice. "Whatever these soulless are, I think they're on their way. If you know where this place is, let's go...now."

"I have an idea, but I'm not certain," Monty said as he traced symbols in the air. "A mistake can be costly."

"If we stay here, we're going to have to face whatever is coming," I said, looking into the night around us. "I'm not a fan of facing something that goes by the name of soulless. We go with your idea."

Anu nodded and Peaches whined next to my leg.

"It's unanimous," I continued. "Make with the finger wiggle."

Monty formed a large green circle and traced a gesture in the air.

"Get in," Monty said as his breath frosted. "Now, please."

We stepped into the circle, and Monty placed his hands on the ground while saying some words under his breath. The circle rotated counter-clockwise, glowing a bright green as it turned.

The light became intense, blinding me as the Park disappeared from sight, only to be replaced by a circular stone monument which rested in a small lawn.

The monument was made of black marble, formed in a large circle around gray stone. On the gray stone in the center of the marble circle was etched an image of the world viewed from the north pole. All of the continents were visible, and recessed flood lights illuminated the monument as we walked into the center of the large marble circle.

Anu sat down and breathed out. He focused his gaze on us and nodded.

"This is the place," he said with relief. "How is my friend, Dexter?"

"How did you—?"

"The symbols," Monty finished. "He can see them."

"Yes, I can," Anu said. "Only Dex could create symbols like these. We will have some safety while we are here."

"Safety?" I said looking around. "We're standing outside. How exactly are we safe?"

"Many souls were buried here," Anu said. "It creates"—he interlaced his fingers together—"a barrier against what pursues you. Dex was right in sending you to me."

"I'm not seeing it," I said walking over to a large plaque on one side of the monument. "There's no way this place is a—"

"African Burial Ground National Monument," Anu finished. "As I said, thousands have been buried in these lands. Thousands. This is truly sacred ground, unlike the sands of the Sun Council."

Oh. I remained silent out of respect for the dead.

"My uncle said we have a shadewalker problem," Monty said. "What is a shadewalker?"

Anu nodded and rested both hands on his walking stick before looking at us. He extended one of his hands and rubbed my hellhound's giant head, before saying something under his breath.

Peaches rumbled and let out a low growl before chuffing. Anu smiled and patted Peaches on the head.

"You speak hellhound?" I asked. "What did you say?"

"I merely asked him if he had eaten recently," Anu said. "Hellhounds are notorious for their appetites. He proceeded to inform me that he is currently starving—which only means he is eating regularly. One can never believe a hellhound when it comes to meat."

"Starving, really?" I said looking at my liar of a hellhound. "You ate three enormous sausages not that long ago."

"Which one of you has joined hands with death?" Anu said. "You are both deathtouched, but one of you is the cause, and the other bears the symptom. I would like to know which is which."

"Excuse me, what?" I said. "Joined hands with who?"

"Death?" Anu said looking from Monty to me. "You must be familiar with this term. He is universal across planes and all realities; he is the one constant. Death, Nergal, Mabul, Ahimoth, Orcus, Ajal, Kek, Ankou, Archemoros, Mara, Pana, Azrael, Shivani? Those are just off the top of my head. We could be here all night with all the names he has."

"Azrael," I said, "but we call him Ezra. Actually, he told us to call him Ezra."

"How familiar. You *speak* to him?" he asked. "I suppose that *is* possible if you joined with him. I have never referred to him as Ezra. That is a peculiar name. Are you certain this is the name he gave you?"

"At his deli, yes," I said. "He makes the best pastrami sandwiches in the city."

Anu stared at me, crossed his arms, and he shook his head.

"Your jests are in poor taste," he said. "You are dealing with a serious situation. A shadewalker stalks you, and you find this amusing? I am trying to help you and you are making jokes?"

"I'm not joking," I said. "Monty, tell him."

"He speaks the truth," Monty said. "Azrael requested we call him Ezra and he currently owns an establishment that prepares food."

"He must be monumentally bored if he is doing this," Anu said, surprised, before turning to me. "Why did he join hands with you?"

"We didn't join hands," I said. "I don't even know what that means."

"You are deathtouched," Anu said, pointing at me. "Why and for how long?"

"Ezra didn't give me a death touch. We haven't so much as shaken hands," I said. "I don't know what you're talking about."

"Ah, but you have done more than shake hands," Anu said, narrowing his eyes at me. "You have been cursed alive, have you not?"

"Kali? You mean Kali?"

Anu cocked his head to one side and gave me a look that said: *I'm this close to slapping you upside your head.*

"Kali is the goddess of?" Anu asked. "You truly do not know? You have been marked."

"I just never...I mean, I never connected...Kali is a goddess, and Ezra is—"

"And your bondmate—am I to assume that you are not aware that his scion serves another personification of Death? Hades, as you may know him?"

I sat down and caught my breath.

"It would seem this was news," Anu said. "You have been surrounded by Death for some time now. This is how I know you are the deathtouched. You have been inextricably linked with death. No wonder Kish was agitated; you weren't just cursed to him; you represented—"

"Anathema," Monty finished. "The foulest being that could ever exist."

"More or less accurate," Anu said with a nod. "And he carries a weapon of desecration. May I see it?"

I looked at him with a blank expression. For a few seconds my brain was misfiring. I recognized the words, but I couldn't really comprehend what he was asking me.

"Ebonsoul," Monty said. "He wants to see Ebonsoul."

"Oh, Ebonsoul, sure," I said, gathering my thoughts. "Sorry, I'm still trying to put this all together."

"I promise to explain it to you as best as I can," Anu said, looking around the monument. "We should be safe for some time still. The shadewalker stalking you"—he glanced at Monty—"hasn't acquired the totem it seeks. May I see your weapon?"

I focused and created a silver mist in my hand. With another effort of focus, Ebonsoul formed in my hand.

"It is exquisite," Anu said, looking at Ebonsoul warily. "May I hold it?"

I turned Ebonsoul around and handed it to him hilt first. The runes along its blade pulsed softly with red, violet, gold, and white energy. I noticed the black energy was missing, but I didn't mention it.

"Be careful," I said. "It's been runed so many different ways, I'm afraid it might explode one day."

"Perfectly balanced," Anu said as he hefted the blade and closed his eyes. "This is a necrotic seraph, one that is a siphon as well as the repository of a powerful being. Each one of these states alone make this weapon dangerous, but combined? This is what the shadewalker wants. This is a key."

"A key?"

"Can you explain?" Monty said. "How is his weapon a key?"

"A shadewalker is created from hatred, regret, knowledge, and the darkness of necromancy," Anu said, staring at Monty and pointing at him. "Things that have been roaming freely within you, mage."

"I bear no one ill will," Monty said. "There is no hatred within me."

"Perhaps not toward others," Anu said gently, "but what about toward yourself? How do you feel about yourself? Do you approve of the mage you've become?"

"I don't think about it," Monty said quickly. "I am who I am, what I am."

"I see," Anu said. "As I was saying, a shadewalker needs a source...animosity, hatred, an unresolved conflict. Do you possess any of these, Mage Montague?"

"Doesn't everyone?" Monty said. "None of us is perfect. We all have regrets and things we would undo if we could."

"True," Anu said. "Not all of us have soulless stalking us, though. Someone from your past chases you. They chase you because of something that happened with him"—he pointed at me—"and that blade."

"Someone from my past," Monty asked. "Someone dead, an old sect mate."

"Not just dead," Anu said. "Someone killed by your hand."

Monty narrowed his eyes at Anu.

"This is true, I have seen him," Monty said. "One of the many that have died by my hands, casts, and words."

"I do not know how many that has been," Anu said shaking his head. "But I am certain you do."

"You do?" I asked, shocked. "You've kept count?"

"Every life matters," Monty said his voice low. "It doesn't matter if they were trying to kill me or mine, it's still a life, no matter how twisted they were. They deserve to be remembered."

"That must be some burden," Anu said, "One you must have been carrying for some time."

"It is mine to carry," Monty said. "It forms part of the cost I must pay to be who I am."

"I think I understand now," Anu said. "You bear this cost willingly, as all mages do, but you also feel responsible for the victims, for those who tried to end your life."

"They fell in battle while trying to end *my* life," Monty explained. "They fell by my hand. I am responsible."

"You are not, but feel you are," Anu said. "This is where your shadewalker is born, in this feeling. The strongest of your regrets gave birth to this shadewalker. You find that, and you find the source."

"Are you trying to say—?"

"Nothing," Anu said, holding up a hand. "I am merely explaining a shadewalker. It needs the power that has been formed in you, along with a key to be released. If soulless are present, a shadewalker commands them. It is only a matter of time before it searches for a key." He hefted up Ebonsoul. "This is a powerful key and one connected to the both of you. It would be perfect."

"How do we stop this shadewalker?" I asked, extending my hand as Anu returned Ebonsoul, and absorbing it a second later. "Can we stop it?"

"Yes," Anu said. "You must locate its corpse road and undo the curse."

TWENTY-TWO

"Locate a corpse road?" I asked. "What exactly is a corpse road? I'm going to take a guess and say that this road isn't shown on any map, right?"

Anu shook his head.

"This is no conventional road," he said. "Who is the shadewalker?"

I turned to Monty and realized that the area around the monument had become darker, buried in shadow. The area where we were was clear, but the space around us seemed to be dimmed, and growing darker.

"Are the soulless here?" I asked taking in the deeper night around us. "Is that why—?"

"Yes," Anu said and gestured, before striking the ground three times with his walking stick. "This will halt their progress, but it will not stop them entirely. Mage Montague, who is the shadewalker?"

"Do you even know?" I asked. "I mean, are you certain? You said it yourself, there have been so many. Maybe it's someone you don't remember?"

"He remembers," Anu said staring at Monty. "This would

be a death of regret, a death you wish you could undo. One that occurred when you were young, well, younger. A boy perhaps."

Monty nodded.

"Taylor," Monty said and the darkness around us rippled. "Cavan Taylor."

Anu kept his gaze on the darkness and nodded.

"It would seem this Taylor is attuned to you both," Anu said and turned to me. "How did this happen?"

"You're asking *me*?" I said flabbergasted. "How am I supposed to know?"

"You are the deathtouched," Anu said. "You are supposed to know. He is the target, but you...you are the cause. You and your blade."

"So now this is my fault?"

"I did not say that."

"You implied it," I said. "Yes, I may be deathtouched, but I did not bring Taylor back."

"I never said you did," Anu said. "Shadewalkers travel between worlds. Normally the barriers between the living and dead are stable and there is no interaction. Sometimes, in the case of a wrongful death, a remnant of the soul remains. That remnant becomes the shadewalker if given what it needs to make the transition."

"I gave Taylor what he needed?" I asked. "Even without knowing him? How is that possible?"

"I'm going to need to you to take a deep breath and calm down," Anu said. "Panicking is not going to be of any use."

"I'm not panicking. Does it sound like I'm panicking? I mean, it's bad enough with some of the things we face regularly," I pointed out. "Now we're facing soulless things? How do you get rid of something that has no soul?"

"You do sound a little panicked," Anu said, pinching his

fingers together. "You dispatch the soulless by bringing rest to the shadewalker."

"How dangerous are the soulless?" I asked. "I mean— really, what are they, ghosts?"

Anu stood and stepped to the edge of the marble floor. He stood right up against the growing darkness, which was now moving and swaying like an ocean wave against a wall of energy.

It was eerie and disturbing to look at, but I had a hard time pulling my eyes away. Anu pulled his sleeve back and thrust his arm into the darkness.

"The soulless seek one thing above all others," Anu said, staring at me. "There is one thing that drives them relentlessly—life."

He pulled his arm back, revealing it to be wrinkled and aged. It looked like it belonged to a mummy.

"They feed on life?"

"Life force to be precise," Anu said with a wince as his arm slowly returned to normal. "Now, why do *you* think the soulless are here, deathtouched?"

"Well, shit," I said. "I may as well be waving a sign saying all-you-can-eat dinner."

"Crude, but accurate," Anu said, rolling down his sleeve. "It's not just you. It's both of you. This shadewalker is tethered to Mage Montague; think of the soulless as a byproduct of its presence. They wish you no harm, but if you fall into their hands, they will never let you go."

"And the shadewalker?" Monty asked. "Taylor is not harmless."

"No," Anu said. "He wants life, and will try to use the key to return, but shadewalkers always have a target. In this case, that would be you, Mage Montague. He will blame you for his death, no matter how much of a hand he had in its happening."

"It should have just been Gwell," Monty said. "Taylor was a confused child, we both were. He was in the wrong place at the wrong time."

"Why doesn't this happen more often?" I asked, turning the situation over in my head. "Why aren't there more shade-walkers roaming around if it just has to do with wrongful deaths, hatred, regret, knowledge, and darkness?"

"Not just any darkness," Anu said. "The darkness of necromancy. This Taylor—was he, or any of his instructors, a necromancer?"

"He was a deathcaster," Monty said. "Bloody hell, Gwell was one of his instructors. He was a necromancer too."

Anu nodded.

"And now you have Simon Strong, the deathtouched bearer of a necrotic blade," he said, pointing at me. "Like calls to like."

"I'm not a necromancer," I protested. "There is no like calling like here at all. Tell him, Monty."

"It makes sense," Monty said, rubbing his chin. "My uncle implied as much."

"Dexter was always attuned to death—in his own way."

"Why didn't I see it earlier?"

"You would have never seen it, if not for Strong's blade," Anu said. "I am afraid our time draws short. I must return to my plane soon."

"Return?" I said, confused. "Aren't you going to help us fight the soulless and this shadewalker?"

"I just have," Anu said. "I have given you the most potent weapon you can wield: knowledge."

"Knowledge is great, but I was hoping for some kind of soulless-remover," I said, staring at the surrounding darkness. "Maybe something to convince the shadewalker to go home?"

Anu smiled and shook his head.

"If Dexter sent you to me, it was to equip you to face this

entity," he said. "Not fight it for you. Besides, I cannot face *your* shadewalker. You two must face and dispatch this creature. I cannot do it for you."

"But you stopped the soulless," I said, pointing at the darkness. "Can you give Monty the anti-shadewalker cast?"

"Only Mage Montague knows that," Anu said. "I have opened your eyes to another dimension—one you may have been aware of, but did not see clearly. Now you can see it better."

"Honestly, I could have lived my entire life without seeing this dimension better," I said. "Now I'm going to go around seeing dead people?"

"Possibly," Anu said. "But there is nothing to fear. Your life is a weapon against the soulless—use it well."

"My life is the weapon? What does that mean?"

"I must depart," Anu said and hit the ground again with his walking stick, forming a large orange circle in the center of the marble floor of the monument. "Sacred grounds are safe for short periods. Do not let the soulless overwhelm or surround you. Their presence creates a dampening field."

"How strong of a field?" Monty asked. "What casts will it stop?"

"Strong enough to prevent you from casting anything but the most basic of casts," Anu replied, looking around. "You must not tarry here long after I leave, or you will be trapped within the monument."

"I'm not exactly seeing an exit here," I said. "How do we stop Taylor?"

"You must confront and dispel Taylor," he answered. "Every shadewalker has a truth they will not confront; it's usually a mirror of the truth within the target. Force him to confront his and it will allow you to stop him. He will approach you soon. Find his corpse road and face him there."

"Will he possess the same abilities he had while he lived?" Monty asked. "Are we facing a deathcaster?"

"Yes, Montague," Anu answered. "You and his corpse road are his weakness. You can fight him anywhere, but you can only defeat him there—on the road."

"How do we find his corpse road?" I asked. "And what did you mean, by my life is a weapon? Why do mages always speak in riddles?"

"Infuriating, isn't it?" Anu said with a short laugh. "Let me do my best with the little time I have. Like you, I am not a mage, and your life-force is a weapon—use it as you have been taught."

"Oh, my life force. Now that you explain it that way, it actually makes sense."

"It does?" Monty asked, looking from me to Anu with confusion. "Really?"

"A corpse road is not an actual road in this context, but is rather the path you must travel to reconcile the wrongful death," Anu said. "The first step in finding it is to go back to the beginning of that death.

"The beginning of the wrongful death leads to the corpse road," I said, seeing the pieces fall into place. "I get it now."

"You do?" Monty asked confused. "How? What exactly are you getting? And why am I not seeing this?"

"Above all," Anu continued, "whatever you do, you must not allow Taylor to get the key you hold."

"You understood what he said?" Monty asked.

"Yes, you didn't?"

"Perhaps I spoke too plainly," Anu said, looking into the night. "Think on my words, Mage Montague and they will become clear to you, as they have for Strong."

"Thanks for not using magespeak," I said. "If only every mage spoke this plainly. My life would be much easier."

"The shadewalker approaches," Anu said, looking into the

night. "He is not at full strength, not yet, but he still poses a threat. Face him with the utmost care. I have full confidence in you three. Give my regards to Dex, and I hope we meet again in the future."

The orange circle rotated clockwise and grew brighter as Anu stepped into the center.

With a bright flash, he disappeared.

TWENTY-THREE

"He left us with more questions than answers," I said. "Are we supposed to get this Taylor some afterlife therapy sessions? How do we get him to confront a truth he doesn't want to confront?"

"Look," Monty said pointing into the night. "He's getting closer."

I didn't think it was possible, but the night became darker as the temperature around the monument dropped. Frost formed on the marble wall, and ice covered the trees surrounding the stone circle.

"Tristan Montague," a voice hissed into the night. "Finally."

"It's never a good sign when voices like that say things like *finally*," I said. "It usually means they've been at this for some time, and are now pissed and frustrated."

"Somewhat dramatic, don't you think, Taylor?" Monty said, turning in the direction of the voice. "What do you want?"

"What do I want... What do I want?" Taylor's disembodied voice said. "I want what's rightfully mine. I want the life you stole from me!"

"I did no such thing," Monty snapped. "You listened to Gwell. You plotted to attack me. You bought into his lies. You allowed him to execute his deception by switching the program you were working on—life extension, bollocks! You tried to kill me!"

"You egotistical, entitled, arrogant snob," Taylor shot back. "You pranced about the Golden Circle, the prince of the Montagues who could do no wrong. The mage prodigy, so special, so gifted. The rest of us weren't worthy enough to breathe the same air as you. You disgust me!"

"I can assure you, the feeling is mutual," Monty said, taking a few steps back. "Why not return from whence you came? No one misses you here."

The darkness coalesced and formed a figure at the edge of the monument. It stepped forward and stopped, pressing a hand against an invisible barrier. All around the figure, the darkness rippled and flowed.

He was dressed in a typical black mageiform—though with a deep violet shirt and a lavender tie, which he somehow made work. The edges of his body flowed into the liquid darkness around him, blending in with the greater darkness surrounding us.

"That's not creepy at all," I said, keeping my voice low. "You're Taylor? I thought you'd be taller."

"And you're inconsequential," Taylor answered, dismissing me with a look before turning to Monty. "Montague, these barriers won't stop me for much longer. My soulless are feeding me even as we speak. Soon, I will be able to cast, and when I do, I will end your miserable existence."

"How about we don't wait until he can cast?" I said, keeping my eyes on the flowing darkness around Taylor. "Why don't we strike him now?"

"I'm in complete favor of that plan," Monty said. "There are, however, two obstacles:.he's behind that barrier, and I haven't the slightest idea on how to begin attacking him."

"Wonderful," I said, still looking at Taylor and the soulless. "In the meantime, he gets stronger and has these soulless giving him energy?"

"It appears so," Monty said. "We also have a more immediate concern."

"More immediate than all this darkness and your long-lost bud itching to take us out?" I asked. "Because that seems pretty immediate to me at this moment."

"Whatever deterrent Anu used to keep the soulless at bay is weakening along the south wall. Once that falls we will be attacked by them," he said. "That, however, is not the main concern."

"Finger-wiggle a circle and let's get the hell out of Dodge," I said, glancing at the south barrier wall. "The sooner the better."

"That would be the immediate concern," Monty said as he gestured. Symbols appeared in front of him and evaporated. "I can't cast."

"You can't what?"

"You heard me," Monty said, reaching behind him and coming up empty. "I can't access the Sorrows either. It would seem this dampening field is targeted at me. Fascinating."

"No! Not fascinating," I nearly yelled. "Disastrous, horrible, very bad—anything but fascinating, Spock!"

"Calm down," Monty said. "There is a solution. Anu wouldn't leave us here defenseless. Think—what did he say?"

"You want me to recall everything he said? Are you insane?"

"Not everything, just the parts regarding the soulless," he said. "Do you recall?"

I took a deep breath and gathered my thoughts. The

rippling darkness and the smiling Taylor were not helping my recall.

"Futile," Taylor said. "This barrier will fall, and my soulless will claim you. Then I will find a key and open a doorway into your world. It's only a matter of time, Montague."

"Not if I have anything to say about it," Monty said. "Simon, ignore him. Think about what Anu said."

"Yes, by all means, ignore me...Simon, is it?" Taylor mocked. "I'm only waiting around to devour your life. Why are you even here? Is this your lackey, Montague? Have you taken on an apprentice?"

He narrowed his eyes and stared at me.

"One moment...you're no mage," Taylor continued, as a wicked smile crossed his lips. "I see. You...you hold my key. You are a conduit. Oh, this is exquisite. I have you both within my grasp. My enemy and my savior. I'm going to enjoy seeing you both die and give me new life. I promise you Tristan—the last thing you will experience will be me snuffing the life from your body as I enter this world."

"Simon, focus," Monty said, snapping his fingers in my face. "Forget him. Look at me. What did Anu say? Something about your life being a weapon. Think."

"You don't remember?" I shot back. "You were there with me."

"This dampening field isn't just a dampening field," Monty said, looking around. "It's impacting my ability to concentrate on anything complex for more than a few seconds. I'm going to need you to really focus here."

"It's getting a little hard to focus when Taylor the Terror over there is threatening to exterminate us," I said, shaking my head and trying to recall Anu's words. "Anu said...my life is a weapon, and to use it. That's pretty much all he said."

"Your life is a weapon, use it?" Monty echoed. "Use it?"

The barrier along the south side of the monument, which had appeared solid a few minutes ago, was beginning to do an excellent imitation of Swiss cheese. Large holes were appearing, and the soulless were beginning to pour in.

We started backing up as the inky darkness slowly began flowing into the monument space.

"Monty, this is the moment when you have an amazing insight," I said, keeping my gaze fixed on the darkness in front of us. "You know, the square of the quantum field extrapolated by the sum of the energy coefficient allows for the manipulation of the ambient energy all around us. You know, the way you usually speak."

"I sound nothing like that. You're speaking gibberish," he said, and then I saw his expression as it clicked. "In fact, the only time you make sense with energy is when you use your magic missile. That's it—cast your missile!"

"My missile?"

"Yes, Simon, and doing so now would be excellent," Monty said as we backed up even more. "At the gap would be ideal." He pointed in front of us. "Right there, next to Taylor, but do not hit him. Do not use your blade. This should work. The dampening field isn't keyed to you."

I aimed my hand at the gap next to Taylor and took a deep breath, focusing my energy, gathering it inside.

"*Ignis vitae!*" I yelled as a large blast of red, violet, and golden energy left the palm of my hand and crashed right into the gap where I was aiming. Screams of agony filled the night as the blast evaporated the soulless.

"No!" Taylor screamed along with the soulless as he vanished from sight. "I *will* have my vengeance, Montague!"

The rest of the soulless dispersed, but they didn't disappear entirely—they moved to the outer edges of the monument. Monty gestured with a new clarity on his face and formed a large green circle. He grabbed me and Peaches and whispered a word under his breath.

The monument disappeared in a green flash.

TWENTY-FOUR

"What the hell was that?" I asked when we arrived at the entrance of the Randy Rump. Jimmy had noticed the green flash and walked over to where we stood. "Monty?"

Monty took several steps and stumbled forward. I managed to catch him with an assist from Jimmy. He brought him farther into the Rump and headed straight for the back room.

The patrons around us gave us concerned glances for a few seconds, then went back to their conversations, mostly ignoring us. It was the Randy Rump crowd, after all. They had seen this place get blown up, obliterated, and attacked by all kinds of creatures multiple times. Monty and me stumbling in was probably the lowlight of the evening. They were most likely waiting for something cataclysmic to happen. Even though it was an official neutral zone, it had actually become an unofficial badge of honor to survive a dining experience at the Randy Rump and not end up in Haven for dessert.

I noticed a few shirts that read: *I survived a night in the Randy Rump* as we passed the tables and headed to the back. I ignored most of the stares, even though the majority of the looks were directed at my hellhound, who had become something of a minor neighborhood celebrity.

There were a few hushed, "*Peaches, that's him, the hellhound!*" in the background as we crossed the floor to the massive door that closed off the backroom.

With a few presses on the runes inscribed on the Buloke door, Jimmy got it open and ushered us inside. He placed Monty on one of the large sofas and stared at me.

"How bad is it?" Jimmy asked, then held up a finger. "Hold that thought—be right back."

He left the back room and sealed the door behind him. It was the first time I had noticed that he had sealed the door with us inside.

"Prudent," Monty said, slowly sitting up. "He's finally acting like the overseer of a neutral zone. Assess and neutralize the threat whenever possible. At this moment, he should be evacuating the restaurant, ensuring the safety of the patrons, and enacting some sort of emergency protocols, as he activates the new defensive runes to ensure the building stays intact."

"What was with the brain fog?" I asked. "I've never seen a dampening field have that effect on you. What happened?"

"That brain fog, as you call it, was a calculated attack," Monty said. "One of the easiest ways to neutralize any magic user is to attack the mind. Without the mind"—he tapped his temple—"you have no casting."

"That was too close," I said. "We can't roam the streets. Do you think the soulless are headed this way?"

"Eventually, yes," he said. "I don't think these defenses are designed to deal with entities that lack life."

"They're undead?"

"Closer to unalive," Monty said, rubbing his chin. "We need to decipher the method Anu gave us to defeat Taylor."

"Is that really Taylor?" I asked. "You said you killed him."

"I did, or at least I thought I did," Monty said. "He was a deathcaster, and Gwell was an advanced necromancer. Could they have cheated death somehow?"

"Death and necromancers," I said. "I don't know. From what we've dealt with, necromancers know how to avoid dying."

"Unfortunately, I think you may be right," Monty said. "Somehow, Gwell must have released a cast that allowed Taylor to avoid a complete death, a cast that shunted him into becoming a shadewalker."

"Is that possible?"

"I'm not a shadewalker," Monty said. "I don't possess enough information about this, but we know someone who does."

"We do?"

"Actually we have two options," Monty said. "I don't think you will like either."

I was about to ask who, but the runes on the door blazed with orange energy when Jimmy activated them and opened the door again. He came in with a tray of food, as well as coffee for me and tea for Monty. In the other hand, he held a large titanium bowl with a large letter P etched into one side, which was filled with prime pastrami.

He placed the tray on the large conference table and put the bowl for Peaches on the floor near the table. I nodded to my hellhound, who bounded over to the meat and stuffed his face into the bowl.

"Don't inhale it," I called out as I grabbed the large mug of Death Wish. "Slow down."

Monty walked over to the table and took the steaming cup of Earl Grey tea. He brought it up to his face and inhaled the aroma with a groan of satisfaction before taking his first sip.

"Thank you, James," Monty said. "This will work wonders."

Jimmy had resealed the door and now stood in front of it with his arms crossed. The look on his face was determined. We weren't leaving the Rump without an explanation.

"Now, tell me how bad it is," Jimmy said. "And what happened to you? You forgot how to teleport? You looked a bit shaky on arrival there."

"I was dealing with the effects of a dampening field," Monty said after taking a long pull of his tea. "Restricted my casting and tampered with my mind."

"This dampening field addled your brain?"

"Something along those lines," Monty said. "It was unexpected. I'll have to take measures to shield my mind to prevent that from happening again in the future. Did you evacuate—?"

"The Rump is empty," Jimmy said. "Grohn activated the defenses and bunkered down. We put out a call to the Dark Council that we're running silent, which means no neutral activities for the duration of the evening."

"You have a designation for something like that?" I asked. "That makes sense, actually, considering the number of Randy Rump renovations."

"Especially after the number of times you two have either had a hand in the renovation, or someone who wanted to crush you managed to renovate the Rump in the process of said attempted crushing."

"I'm really sorry about that," I said, and meant it, before I took a long pull of my Death Wish. "Each and every time it happens, I want you to know it's not on purpose. No hard feelings?"

"None. We're a neutral zone," Jimmy said, patting Peaches on the head. "Granted, we see more action than most neutral zones in the city combined, but we're supposed to be here for people who need help—all people, not just a select few. Those of us in the supernatural community have few places to run to when we're in trouble. It just happens that the trouble that follows you three around is armageddon-sized."

"We do apologize," Monty said. "We will repair any damages and restore any of the damaged runework."

"I know you will," Jimmy said with a smile. "Or the Director of the Dark Council has promised to have a conversation with you"—he pointed at me—"for the repeated destruction of a neutral zone. You do not want to get on that vampire's bad side, trust me."

"Michiko said that?"

"I have it in writing in my office," he said. "She even created the designation code for your emergency visits. She calls them a T3 Terror Event—or T3TE."

"You're serious?" I asked. "We have our own code?"

"I have a direct line to the Council HQ," he said with a nod. "I say that code and we are on lockdown. A DCE mixed force will be down here in ten minutes to clear a perimeter several blocks away. Reduces collateral damage."

"Wow," I said. "I didn't know they had put something like that in place."

"Turns out the Dark Council doesn't appreciate having their neutral zone blown to bits," Jimmy said. "Now, what are we facing?"

"We?" Monty said. "We can't be here—"

"I can and I will," Jimmy said, untying the apron which read *I'm Unbearable*. "What's after you and where are you going?"

"Soulless," Monty said. "Do you know what they are?"

"No, but they don't sound friendly."

"We can't stay," Monty said. "They are after us. As their name indicates, they possess no soul and feed off life-force. You can't face them."

"But *you* can?" Jimmy asked upset. "Why? Do you have extra-life or something?"

"He doesn't, but I do," I said. "I'll explain when we have more time."

"Which means never," Jimmy said. "You can use my help."

"Listen, I would totally want you to stand with us against this threat, but not if it means losing you. These things will age you into death in seconds. Can your werebear form withstand something like that?"

"No," Jimmy admitted. "Werebears aren't designed to face life siphons. We can deal with magic users, having a supernatural null component to our nature, but we still have life force. These soulless could attack me."

"And they would," Monty said with a nod. "We must leave before they track us down."

"You think they can?" I asked. "They didn't seem that aware when we ported out of there."

"You had just hit them with your magic missile," Monty said. "It must have disoriented them, but it's not the soulless that concern me. Taylor can find us, and if he can find us—"

"The soulless can," I finished with a heavy sigh. "Wonderful."

"Taylor?" Jimmy asked. "Who's Taylor?"

"Someone from Monty's past who he killed, but not entirely. He wants revenge, but first he has to siphon my life and steal my blade to create a passage back into this world. Once he does that, he can come back completely and kill Monty," I said and glanced at Monty. "Did I leave anything out?"

"No, I think that pretty much covers everything," Monty said after drinking the rest of his tea. "The soulless and Taylor are getting stronger. We need to stop him, but first we need to make one stop."

"Right, the two options," I said. "We know someone who

can deal with shadewalkers, or at least decrypt what Anu told us?"

"Yes," Monty said. "We can go speak to Badb Catha or—"

"No, absolutely not," I said without letting him finish. "First, Dex said that was a Bad Idea. Second, you've never spoken to her, and on top of that, she and I have some kind of understanding. I owe her."

"I'm aware," Monty said. "There's a fifty-year leave of absence in our future."

"I told you, you didn't have to do it."

"Your choice saved my life," Monty said. "Fifty years of service is a small price to pay."

"Well, we're not starting that anytime soon, so Badb Catha is a hard no," I said. "Who's the other option?"

"Hades."

"Oh, hell, really?"

"Quite literally in this case," Monty said and began to gesture. "Are you ready?"

"What, now?"

"Each second that passes, Taylor grows stronger," Monty said as he focused on the circle forming in front of us. "We can't waste time."

"You may as well leave the T3TE thing in place," I said, looking at Jimmy. "That way, if the soulless head this way you'll have some warning."

I extended an arm, which Jimmy grabbed by the forearm. I did the same to him, except my hand barely wrapped around his arm, and his massive hand nearly enveloped my entire forearm.

"You three be safe out there," he said. "I'll hold your table for you."

"We have a table?" I asked. "Since when?"

"Since I reserved the corner table for you three," Jimmy

said. "You know the corner I mean. It's the one you keep blowing to bits."

I knew exactly which table he meant.

"I know the table. Hey, thanks—really."

"It was more a matter of no one else wanting to sit in that corner," he said with a shrug. "Something about strange dangerous vibes of destruction and death."

"Thank you, again, James," Monty said and shook his hand. "I do hope we can visit one day without impending death pursuing us."

"I'd like that, too," Jimmy said and stepped back. "Good luck."

He rubbed Peaches' head and reminded him to be a good boy. Peaches chuffed and nudged his leg, nearly knocking him over.

<Tell the bear man I said thank you for the meat. It was very good.>

"He's saying thank you for his bowl of meat," I said, rubbing my hellhound's enormous head as he stood next to me. "See you soon."

Jimmy nodded.

"I hope so," Jimmy said before moving back a few more steps. "Watch your six."

"Always," I said as the Randy Rump disappeared in a violet cloud of energy and the floor rotated sideways. "Oh, this is going to suck."

TWENTY-FIVE

We arrived in Hades.

"You left my stomach in the Randy Rump," I said as I doubled over. Several waves of nausea gripped me and it took everything I had not to lose my lunch. "Was that really necessary?"

"Teleportation to Hades is never straightforward," Monty said. "Actually, I'm quite surprised we made it...intact, that is."

"You expected us to explode on the way here?"

"I expected some kind of resistance," he said, looking around. "But we're here. Hades must have facilitated some sort of passage for you to access this place freely."

I stared at him for a few seconds before another wave of nausea gripped me and twisted my stomach into knots.

"Ugh, this is horrible," I said, gripping my midsection. "I thought I was done with this."

"Breathe. The discomfort should pass soon," he said. "Do you recognize where we are?"

We were standing in a grassy area covered with all kinds of flowers. Trees formed small groves all around us, which were separated by clear running brooks winding their way through the trees.

"This is Orethe's home. We're in Elysium," I said. "I thought you were taking us to see Hades."

The small familiar cottage, encircled by a short fence, was just over a small hill as we advanced. The front of the cottage was simple: a plain wooden door, which I noticed now was covered in intricate runes, faced us, and on the stone patio a large rocking chair was resting.

"Not Orethe's home any longer," Monty said. "Remember? This is now your home."

Behind the cottage there was another brook that fed into a large garden. On either end of the small cottage I saw windows which gave it a cozy feel. We approached the home and waited on the patio.

"How exactly is this my home if I can't access it?"

"What do you mean?" Monty said, glancing behind us. "She left this home and everything inside of it to you, along with all the necrotic information contained within your blade."

"The blade I understand," I said, nodding. "I can try and access the information in there, or get your or the Morrigan's help with that. How am I supposed to get here, to the home? It's not like I can create a teleportation circle."

"Hmm. That is a good point," Monty said. "Perhaps with your creature you can form a method to get here easily. He does step in-between. It's possible he may have a way to access Elysium and bring you along."

A wave of energy raced over me and I looked at Monty in surprise.

"Was that—?"

"No," Monty answered. "Hades."

"Where?" I said, looking around. The cottage was on the

small side. If Hades was nearby, we would be able to see him easily unless he was—"Inside?"

Monty nodded and headed for the door.

We entered the small cottage.

A strong sense of disorientation washed over me as the immense size of the interior expanded before us.

The interior of the cottage was difficult to process.

No matter how many times I had witnessed the weird stretching of time and relative dimension in space, it always caught me off-guard when I stood in the middle of a "cottage" that felt like an aircraft hangar on the inside even though it looked like a closet from the outside.

I slowly took in the interior again. The last time I was here, we were pressed for time and dealing with a revenant. I noticed the trend.

"Do you think we could go somewhere, anywhere, and actually enjoy the place we're visiting?"

"I don't understand," Monty said, walking ahead. "Elaborate."

"I'd like to visit, let's say this cottage, just for the sake of visiting the cottage," I said. "Not because we need to get some information from Hades to defeat Taylor the shade-walker. Does that make sense?"

"Perfect sense," a voice said from around the corner. "You'd like to visit a place like this for enjoyment, not out of necessity."

Hades.

"Yes," I said. "You knew we were here?"

"You are in Hades," he said from a large comfortable chair. "I know the moment you, or anyone for that matter, sets foot in my demesne. I've made sure to keep it as Orethe left it. You may feel free to rearrange anything as you see fit, however; it is your home, after all."

He was dressed in a casual off-white linen Zegna shirt, a

pair of black Armani pants, and comfortable black Armani loafers.

He was, by his standards, dressing down.

I looked around the large space, marveling at the huge interior. Everything was laid out in a modern open floor plan, reminding me of the large lofts in downtown Manhattan.

The wooden floor shone with the indirect sunlight which spilled in through the windows. A large living area dominated the center of the space, with a fully equipped galley kitchen off to one side. Next to the kitchen was a spacious reading area, complete with several bookcases acting as a dividing wall.

I pointed to some of the shelves, which were empty.

"I took the liberty of returning some of the books Orethe had borrowed," Hades said. "Neither of you are quite as advanced as she was in necromancy. The material you would need access to is still on the shelves, and is at your disposal."

I noticed there were still plenty of books on the shelves. The ones I could decipher dealt mostly with necromancy and death.

"Speaking of necromancy," I started as Hades formed a large sausage and fed it to my ever-voracious hellhound.

"You've reached a battle form?" Hades said staring from me to Peaches, who inhaled the sausage. "That is commendable, and so soon. This is excellent progress."

"Let's not hold any battle form celebrations just yet," I said. "The longest I can hold it is twenty seconds and it's the lowest form."

"Still, twenty seconds can mean the difference between life and death," he said. "That is quite the achievement. I did not expect a battle form from you two for at least another five to six—"

"Years?"

"Decades," Hades finished. "The fact that you have

attained even the lowest form bodes well. It took me over two centuries before attaining the highest level, and Cerberus isn't a pup."

"Two centuries?"

"*Over* two centuries," he said. "And I'm significantly more skilled than you, Strong. These things can't be rushed. Now, to what do I owe the pleasure of your presence in Elysium?"

"We have a problem," Monty said and explained what happened with Keeper Gault and our final battle. "Now a shadewalker stalks me..." He glanced at me. "Well, us."

"That *is* a problem," Hades said after giving it some thought. "Who else have you consulted?"

"Anu of Kengir," Monty said. "My uncle said he was an expert on these things."

"Anu isn't an expert, exactly," Hades said. "Though it does make sense for Dexter to send you to him. How is Anu doing these days? Does the Sun Council still want him dead?"

"In the worst way possible," I said. "Sent a full circle after him while we were there."

Hades smiled.

"He never did learn how to get along with the zealots," Hades said with a shake of his head. "Anu is what's known as a custodian of knowledge. He possesses much information on this subject, but it is colored through the lens of time and culture. I'm sure his 'help' was cryptic at best, and an absolute mystery at worst. Yes?"

"Yes," I said, throwing a hand up. "He said plenty, but little of it made sense, at least to me."

"Tristan?" Hades asked, looking over at Monty. "Do you agree with this assessment?"

"I have to agree with Simon. Anu was somewhat obtuse in his explanation of how to deal with the shadewalker," Monty said. "I couldn't comprehend a direct method of attack."

"Really?" Hades said, leaning back in his chair. "You couldn't, or chose not to?"

"What are you implying?" Monty said as anger crept into his words. "Are you saying I deliberately chose not to understand his instructions?"

"Defeating a shadewalker, rare as they are, is not difficult," Hades replied. "If I'm not mistaken, shadewalkers are born of a wrongful death, hatred, regret, knowledge, and the darkness of necromancy."

"That's what Anu said," I said. "Still don't get it entirely but it's making sense."

Monty glared at me.

"Tristan? Do you find that you don't 'get it' either?"

"It's not clear, no," Monty said, but I heard some hesitation in his voice. "He kept alluding to a corpse road."

"Ah," Hades said. "I think I see the difficulty. Allow me to clarify things for you—but before I do, are soulless involved?"

"Yes," I said. "They're dangerous."

"Quite," Hades said. "Capable of instant aging, if memory serves. How did you confront them?"

"My magic missile," I said. "It can keep them away."

"Tristan? Did you have a method of dealing with the soulless?"

"No, I did not."

"Why not?"

"The dampening effect interfered with my thought processes, making casting impossible," Monty answered after a pause. "It made it all but impossible to think, much less cast."

"I see," Hades said. "And you've come here for *what*, exactly? Clarity of thought?"

"We need to stop this shadewalker," I said. "He wants us dead—"

"We both know that's not possible, not in your current

condition," Hades answered. "He must want something else from you, Strong."

"He wants Ebonsoul," I said. "It's a key. That I know for sure. Called me a conduit, but didn't elaborate more than that. He definitely wants Monty dead."

"When you killed him," Hades said, looking directly at Monty, "the tether between you was in place. It already existed."

"What? Impossible," Monty said. "We were children. He wasn't strong enough to create a tether between us."

"*He* may not have been, but there was a necromancer involved," Hades said. "That necromancer created the tether between the two of you using an artifact. Were you given an item of power before you confronted this shadewalker?"

"Yes," Monty said, giving Hades' words thought, "a shunting disc. It was the only way to create the floating teleport."

"Something your uncle taught you?"

"Yes, but how was the artifact used to create the tether?" Monty asked. "It, too, was given to me by my uncle. Gwell didn't have access to it."

"It's quite possible it contained properties your uncle was unaware of," Hades said. "The necromancer who created the tether utilized the power contained in this shunting disc to create the tether and tie a part of the shadewalker to you. After that, it was only a matter of making sure the other criteria were met."

"Other criteria?" I asked. "What other criteria?"

"A wrongful death, hatred, regret, knowledge, and the darkness of necromancy," Hades said. "I'd say you fulfilled all of the criteria, especially after confronting Keeper Gault."

"Agreed," Monty said with a nod. "Gwell planned this?"

"It would certainly seem so," Hades replied. "Though he probably didn't count on dying with his designated target."

"He was trying to kill Monty and Taylor?"

"Either one would have sufficed to fulfill the wrongful death," Hades said. "This Gwell was after something more—it looks like he was after your uncle. Something must have gone wrong in his cast."

"He hated my uncle," Monty said. "If I had died instead of Taylor—"

"You would have become the shadewalker," Hades finished. "I daresay your uncle would have done anything to reverse your condition at that point. Anything."

"Can the shadewalker be reversed?" I asked. "Can Taylor be saved?"

"Sadly, no," Hades said. "The condition is permanent. You may not be able to reverse it, but you can end it. You must break that tether and confront the shadewalker."

"How do I do that?" Monty asked. "That is the information I require."

"You know how to do that," Hades said. "It's clear."

"To you, perhaps," Monty said. "I am not as versed in the discipline of necromancy as a god of the underworld."

Hades narrowed his eyes and glared at Monty—easily a three, bordering on four on the glare-o-meter.

"You may lie to yourself, but do not lie to me," Hades said with an edge to his voice. "You know what you must do, but you refuse to face this truth. You do not require my expertise or knowledge to carry this out."

Monty looked away.

"He speaks in half-truths and twists his words."

"Then speak in full truths and keep your words straight," Hades said. "Until you do, this shadewalker will stalk you and his soulless will grow in number and power."

"What are you talking about?" I asked. "Why would Monty lie about this?"

"He has his reasons," Hades said, then focused on Monty.

"Know that it's not only you ensnared in this—Strong plays a part as well. The longer you delay, the more danger you will both face."

"You sound just like Anu," I said. "Monty? What is he talking about?"

"The truth and the corpse road," Monty said, getting to his feet and looking at Hades. "Will you grant us passage home?"

"You may come and go freely from this part of Elysium," Hades said with a nod. "This small section is keyed to Strong. He has access to this, his home, given to him by Orethe, whenever he wants."

"I do?" I asked, surprised. "How?"

"Tristan can bring you, as can your hellhound," Hades said. "At least, until you learn to get here on your own."

"On my own?"

"In time, yes, but right now you have other, more pressing matters to attend to. Isn't that right, Mage Montague?"

Monty nodded and formed a large green circle.

"Simon, we have to go," Monty said with urgency. "I know what we, what I, have to do."

"I'm glad someone does," I said. "This thing we have to do, is it going to be—"

"It's going to be unpleasant, yes, for both of us."

"How did I know that would be your answer?"

"We need to prepare. Let's go."

"Where to?"

"Erik has what I need."

"Hellfire Club?"

"We need to meet with Erik," Monty confirmed. "We need to be ready to confront Taylor, and he has what we need...at the Hellfire vault."

Hades gave Peaches one more pat on the head before standing.

"Strong, come visit when you have a moment," Hades said as we stepped into the circle. "I would like to thoroughly examine your battle form. Perhaps I can help you last longer than twenty seconds."

"That would help," I said. "We could probably get up to a full twenty-five seconds before I pass out."

"We shall see," Hades said. "Walk the entire road, Tristan, and you will see the end of this. One more thing—this shade-walker may not be what it seems. Don't believe everything you see. Look beyond the surface."

"I shall," Monty said, gesturing as the circle increased in brightness. "Thank you."

Hades nodded and Orethe's cottage disappeared.

TWENTY-SIX

We arrived at the Moscow garage, next to the Dark Goat.

"Quickly, before Olga realizes we're here," Monty said, placing a hand on the surface of the Dark Goat, unlocking it and getting in on the passenger side. "Now, Simon."

I opened the rear suicide door for the Mighty Sprawl. My hellhound bounded in and took up the entire back seat in one stretch.

I ran over to the driver's side and slid in, turning on the engine with a throaty roar. Monty gave me three seconds to appreciate and bask in the sound before giving me the signal to get going.

"Does Erik know we're on our way?"

"He will."

I managed to drive out of the garage without Olga blocking our way or throwing up an ice wall to stop us in our tracks.

"How did that happen?" I asked as I sped downtown. "She always knows when we're in the building."

"She knew this time, too," Monty said, showing me his

phone as it rang. The number was Olga's. "She just chose to use a different method to let us know she knew."

He put the call on the Dark Goat's speaker phone.

"Hello, Olga," he said. "I was just going to call you."

"Da. How is Cecelia?"

"She is good—studying and preparing for her exam," Monty said. "She will be ready."

"She *must* be ready," Olga answered. "Stronk, are you helping Cece?"

"I am," I said as she mangled my name with violence. "She will be ready."

"Good," she said. "In two weeks I go visit little Cecelia. I will make sure she learns what she must know to pass test. I will see you both at school, da?"

"Yes," Monty said. "We will see you then."

"This is good. *Do svidaniya*."

She ended the call.

"How is she going to get to the school?" I asked, swerving around traffic. "Dex has that place locked down tight."

"As Cecelia's designated guardian, Dex has given Olga limited access to the school," Monty said, dialing another number as I drove. "She will initiate the bridge and Dex will facilitate her smooth arrival."

The call connected a few seconds later.

"And here I thought this was going to be a good day," Erik said over the line. "To what do I owe the torture? Are we due for another cataclysm?"

"Hello, Erik," Monty said. "I need access to the vault."

"The vault?" Erik said his voice serious. "Whatever for?"

"The shunting disc," Monty said. "I trust it's still in your possession. I'm on my way. We'll be there in—"

"Hold on a second," Erik replied quickly. "You said that under no circumstances, should I give you that artifact. That if you requested it...ever, I was to refuse you as many times as necessary until you understood the message."

"Erik," Monty said, that one word the unsheathing of a sword with the promise of death and pain. "I am facing a shadewalker and perhaps more, along with an ever growing contingent of soulless. I strongly advise you to open the vault, find the disc and provide me with said disc, before we are overrun with soulless."

"Bloody hell," Erik said. "An actual shadewalker? Do you know who it is?"

"Taylor."

"Cavan Taylor?" Erik said his voice filled with dread. "The deathcaster? Gwell's little apprentice?"

"One and the same," Monty said. "I think Gwell may be involved somehow."

"As I recall, they're both dead."

"They were also both necromancers," Monty said. "Necromancers and death...you know how it goes."

"It doesn't, most of the time," Erik said with a slight shudder to his voice. "I hate necromancers."

"Have it ready," Monty said. "Do you have access to it?"

"Yes. Tell me you're in a SuNaTran vehicle," Erik said. "Are you in the Dark Goat?"

"Yes," I said. "Why does that matter?"

"Have you experienced the brain fog effect?" Erik asked. "Did it hit you yet, Tristan?"

"Quite by surprise, yes," Monty said. "I'm going to need a countermeasure."

"I have you covered," Erik answered. "The reason it matters, Strong, is that Cecil has runed all his vehicles for almost every contingency possible. As long as Tristan stays in the Dark Goat, he should be immune to the dampening brain fog, at least until he gets the countermeasure."

"Cecil is amazing," I said. "How would he even know to rune the Dark Goat against this brain fog effect?"

"Cecil is deranged is what he is," Erik said with a small chuckle. "But I'm thankful he's on our side."

"Twenty minutes," Monty said. "See you then."

"See you then," Erik said. "If you have guests trailing you, give me a call."

He ended the call.

"Break it down for me," I said, jumping on the West Side Highway and heading downtown. "What exactly are we facing and why do we need this disc artifact?"

"If what Hades said is correct, the disc is the key to the tether," Monty said. "I destroy the artifact, it severs the tether. That should allow me to confront Taylor and, hopefully, bring him a measure of peace."

"Just by breaking the tether?"

"Not entirely," Monty said with a look out of the passenger-side window. "Some of what Taylor—the shadewalker—said was true. I was an arrogant, entitled, self-absorbed spoiled brat of a mage."

"Some?"

He shot me a sideway glare and looked outside again.

"All of it," he said. "When Taylor needed a friend, I turned him away. The universe and the sect revolved around me, or so I thought."

"So you were a proper asshat?"

"I'm not familiar with the term, but it sounds appropriate," Monty said. "If I had been a better friend, I don't think Gwell would have been able to sink his hooks in Taylor."

"You can't change the past," I said, "but you can reconcile with Taylor and stop him from being a shadewalker. Maybe he can have that measure of peace you mentioned."

"I certainly hope so," he said. "Necromancy and the dark arts are not something I'm overly familiar with."

"Don't look at me," I said. "I'm barely getting the hang of a battle form and can only just manage my magic missile. Dealing with dead mages and their plans is way above my pay grade."

Monty's expression suddenly changed. "Simon, how fast can the Dark Goat go?"

"Huh? Why?"

"We have company," Monty said, as he dialed on his phone. The call connected a few seconds later. "Erik, we have company. Set up the defenses around the vault and meet us at the Harlequin."

He ended the call.

I looked in the rear-view mirror and saw only darkness. Not the normal darkness from driving at night—this was the liquified darkness of the soulless.

Peaches gave off a low rumble and a the small whine.

"What the—? Monty, is that...?"

"Yes, the soulless seem to have found us," Monty said, and gestured. Small golden symbols floated over to his head and sank into his skin. "This is a temporary measure, but it should prevent the dampening brain fog."

I floored the accelerator and raced down the West Side Highway. The darkness fell back as we shot forward.

"How did it find us?"

"Not it—them," Monty corrected. "The soulless act like a remora fish, latching on to a shadewalker, but feeding it energy as well. At some point the shadewalker and the soulless will be independent of each other."

"That sounds like a situation we want to avoid," I said, keeping one eye on the wall of darkness behind us. "Are the people on the street in danger?"

"It seems to be focused on us at the moment," Monty said, looking behind us. "If it loses that focus, that may present a danger to the general populace."

"How far is the vault from the Hellfire Club?"

"The vault is *in* the Hellfire Club, in a sub-basement. Erik will meet us at the Harlequin entrance on street level. Do you remember where it is?"

"Yes, but what about these vault defenses?" I asked as we sped towards the Hellfire Club. "Are they going to be strong enough?"

"The Hellfire Club vault holds some powerful and incredibly dangerous items," Monty said, glancing back every few seconds. "We are leading a mostly unknown entity to its location. I don't know if the Hellfire defenses can withstand an attack by the soulless."

I nodded as I saw the Harlequin entrance about a block away. The entrance was surrounded by a group of seven Harlequin. All of them held their glowing tonfa out, creating a cordon of blue energy around the entrance. Next to the Harlequin, I saw Erik, dressed in a black suit and holding a rune-covered steel case about ten inches long by half as wide and six inches deep.

The runes on the case were glowing and fluctuated every few seconds from bright orange to red to violet.

"Head's up," I said. "Erik's at the entrance."

"Do not stop the car," Monty said as he lowered his window and began gesturing. "When I tell you, slow down slightly and then turn around and head back the way we came."

"The way we came?" I asked in disbelief. "That would mean we would head straight into—"

"We are not dragging the soulless to the Hellfire Club, Simon," Monty said. "Now!"

I pulled hard on the wheel, using the emergency brake to execute a fishtail and cut into the turn. Erik was ready. He threw the steel case as Monty gestured, creating a small green circle to catch the case, pulling it into the Dark Goat.

Erik stepped into the circle of Harlequins and gestured. A blue dome of energy formed over the entrance of the Hellfire Club, covering Erik and the Harlequins, blocking them from view.

I was facing the opposite direction, looking down the narrow, short street into an immense wall of liquid darkness racing our way.

"That looks nasty," I said. "I really hope Cecil factored in the soulless when he runed the Dark Goat."

"Me too," Monty said under his breath. "Go right through it. Don't stop."

I stepped on the gas pedal and pushed the Dark Goat faster. Peaches growled as we punched into the liquid darkness. The world went from night time to driving into a large pool of black ink.

Everything disappeared.

If it wasn't for the roar of the engine, I wouldn't have known we were moving. All sensation of motion was gone; a feeling of weightlessness had wrapped itself around us.

Right up until Taylor stopped us.

We burst out of the liquid darkness and into the outstretched arm of Taylor, who was waiting for us on the other side. It would've been softer to run into the nearby building.

The Dark Goat collided into Taylor, who had slammed a hand down on the hood, causing the rear of the Dark Goat to shoot up into the air as we somersaulted over him, hit the ground on our side, and rolled down the street.

The interior of the Dark Goat lit up with all kinds of runes, which I guessed were keeping us alive as we rolled away from Taylor—the shadewalker who had just managed to stop a car going at least eighty miles per hour with the touch of his hand.

We ended up leaning against a building about two blocks

away from the entrance to the Hellfire Club. After we managed to remove our straps, Monty opened his door, which was now the top of the Dark Goat, and we crept out.

My amazing hellhound blinked out and reappeared outside the Dark Goat. I stepped close to him and pointed at the liquid darkness flowing around Taylor.

<*Whatever you do, boy, don't let that dark water cloud touch you. It's dangerous and can hurt you.*>

<*I will stay away. Is the in-between man angry with you?*>

<*Yes. Don't go no near him either. Stay back from the man and the cloud, unless I tell you to attack him. Stay safe by the car.*>

He chuffed and moved back to sit next to the Dark Goat.

"I told you I would grow stronger, Tristan," Taylor said. "I've come to collect what is due to me."

Monty still held the steel case. I saw him open it, remove something from inside, and place it against his temple. It was a small silver disc etched with runes.

Inside the steel case I saw a larger golden disc that thrummed with a deep vibration when he opened the case. He quickly closed it.

"Once I expose the shadewalker, I'll have a small window of time to release Taylor," he said. "You will need to get to safety."

"What do you mean, expose the shadewalker?" I asked, thrown off. "He's right there. Taylor is the shadewalker... isn't he?"

"Yes and no," Monty said. "I need to draw him out."

"Is your brain oatmeal again?" I asked, pointing at Taylor. "The shadewalker is right there. No drawing out is necessary."

"I'm finally understanding what Anu and Hades meant," Monty said. "I didn't want to face it, but I must."

"I know we have to walk the entire corpse road, but it's not a one-way street."

"When I destroy the artifact, it's going to release an immense amount of energy," he said under his breath. "You need to be inside the vehicle with your creature."

"Where are you going to be?"

He looked down the street.

"Facing my past," he said. "I need to confront this shadewalker."

"Then I'm going with you," I said. "You're not facing him alone."

"No, Simon, if those soulless—"

"If they get hold of you, you're toast," I said, materializing Ebonsoul. "He wants this too, not just you. It's a package deal. I say we give him what he wants and end him."

"You can't face him," Monty said, glancing down at the case. "I don't even know if I can."

"It's not him you need to face, I think," I said, glancing down at Taylor. "Besides, between the two of us, you may be Mr. Wiggle-fingers, but I have a better chance of walking away from a one-on-one with a shadewalker surrounded by soulless."

He looked at me, realizing I was determined to see this to the end.

"Very well," he said, grimly. "Let's walk this corpse road."

TWENTY-SEVEN

"A life and my key," Taylor said, as we approached. "Perfect— you saved me the trouble of hunting down your friends, families, and associates. Thank you."

"You're right, Taylor," Monty said, removing the shunting disc from the steel case and holding it in his hand. The energy from the disc reverberated around us with a deep bass vibration. "I stole your life from you, and I'm here to return it to you. Simon?"

Monty extended a hand without looking at me, and I handed him Ebonsoul.

Taylor took a step back, a look of confusion on his face.

"What are you saying?" Taylor demanded. "What are you doing?"

"This is what you wanted," Monty said, raising Ebonsoul as we kept walking down the street. "My life, and a way back. Here it is."

As we closed the distance to Taylor, the liquid darkness shot past us up the street and surrounded Monty and me, cutting off any escape. A nudge by my leg forced me to look down. An icy block of fear gripped my stomach as I noticed my hellhound was by my side.

<What are you doing? I told you to stay safe by the car.>

<I go where you go.>

<No, boy. This is too dangerous.>

<We are bondmates. I go where you go.>

A low growl followed by a long rumble escaped his throat. There was no way I was going to convince him to stay behind.

"Give me the blade," Taylor said, extending an arm. "I promise to make your death long and painful. It's the least you deserve, after my time as this...this thing."

"Of course," Monty said, with a nod. "I did not make you a shadewalker, Taylor. This was not my doing. That is the truth."

"You killed me," Taylor snarled. "You ended my life."

"That...that is true," Monty said, his voice filled with sadness. "For that I am...for that I truly apologize. There is nothing I can say or do to return to you what you have lost."

"You can die."

"If that's what Taylor really wants then I willingly give him my life."

I placed a hand on Monty's shoulder.

"Are you sure about this?" I asked. "I'm all for making amends, but I'm really not feeling this new seppuku Monty."

"Trust me," Monty said. "I know what I'm doing...I think."

"You think?"

He nodded as we stopped approaching.

"I don't have to ask, you know. I can have my soulless end you now," Taylor said with his arm still outstretched. "Give me the blade. This is my time."

"Of course," Monty said, motioning for me to remain

where I stood while giving me a look that said: *Get ready*. "Just one more thing."

He walked over the remaining distance, still holding the shunting disc in his hand. He had touched the face of the disc in several places and I noticed it was growing brighter.

All around us the liquid darkness flowed, a moving wall of death that was only a few feet away.

"One more thing?" Taylor asked. "What is it?"

"How long?" Monty asked. "How long did you think I would remain deceived, Gwell?"

"Long enough for me to get this!" Taylor dashed forward and grabbed Ebonsoul from Monty's hand. "You have given me the means to open a door and return." He turned to the soulless. "Destroy them!"

Monty glanced my way and mouthed one word—*dawnward*—but I was already moving and had formed the dome of energy around me and Peaches by the time he detonated the artifact.

The golden light concentrated on the disc and exploded outward, forcing the soulless away. I saw a violet-and-red beam of energy that resembled a thick rope stretch tight, begin to fray and split apart, while the soulless shrieked all around us.

The high-pitched sound was excruciating. It sounded like metal being wrenched and torn, while hundreds of people experienced the worst agony all at once.

I saw Peaches crouch down next to me as the sound of the soulless washed over us. My dawnward kept the soulless back. With another scream, Taylor the shadewalker split in two and another, older figure emerged from his side.

The second figure held Ebonsoul—as Taylor, who looked on confusedly, covered his ears and dropped to his knees as the screaming continued.

The soulless kept the screaming going as the older figure

extended Ebonsoul overhead and absorbed all of the darkness. In moments, the soulless were gone, creating a deafening silence.

He gave us a look of pure malice and, with Ebonsoul in hand, he sliced the air, creating a tear in the space directly in front of him, before taking several steps forward and into our reality.

With another downward slash he sealed the tear, separating himself from the world of the shadewalker. Taylor looked on, horrified, staring from Monty to the other figure who I could only assume was Gwell.

"You have served your purpose, child," the older figure said, flexing his fingers. "Your time has ended."

Gwell pointed Ebonsoul at Taylor and blasted him with a beam of black energy. The black energy enveloped Taylor, blocking him from view for a few seconds.

When we could see him again, Taylor was unscathed and surrounded by a golden lattice.

I saw Monty gesture and step forward. As he gestured, a golden tether appeared between him and Taylor.

"You can't harm him, Gwell," Monty said. "It's not your weapon to wield."

"I will use this weapon as I see fit!" Gwell said, holding up Ebonsoul again. "It is mine now. The shadewalker has served his purpose, and will die a final death."

"You've stepped over to this side of the veil," Monty said. "Taylor is beyond your reach now."

"I may not be able to harm him," Gwell said through gritted teeth, "but the soulless can reach him wherever he is. After all, he is pure life-force. Your lattice can only protect him for so long."

Gwell slashed with an arm, and a cloud of soulless vanished from sight.

"Gwell?" Taylor said, still confused. "You promised me...

you promised me power. You said I would be the best necromancer in the sect. You promised! I only had to beat Tristan in the duel, teach him a lesson, and you would help me unlock my next level."

Gwell laughed.

"Stupid, foolish child," Gwell said. "I told you whatever you needed to hear. All I needed was a wrongful death. I had no idea that death would be mine as well." He glanced at Monty, who ignored him. "I underestimated you, Montague."

"Hold still, Taylor," Monty said, looking at Taylor. "My lattice will keep you safe for the time being."

"Keep him safe?" Gwell seethed. "Who's going to keep you safe?"

Gwell pointed Ebonsoul and unleashed a beam of soulless at Monty, who created a shield, deflecting them away. They crashed into a wall and regrouped as Gwell formed several black orbs of energy and released them at us.

<You can bite him, boy—but don't let him hit you with that black energy.>

<Can I take him in-between?>

<No, he's too dangerous to take in-between. He seems to know his way around those places. You can blink in and out, but stay on this plane and don't take him anywhere, I don't want to lose you.>

<You can never lose me. I'm your bondmate.>

Peaches blinked out.

I had a feeling he was right, but I wasn't willing to take a chance with Gwell, who had managed to survive for I don't know how long between worlds.

My hellhound reappeared next to Gwell and pounced. Gwell waved a hand and opened a rift, disappearing my hellhound. I held my breath, every second a lifetime, until I saw him reappear, smashing into Gwell with his massive head, knocking him off his feet.

Gwell recovered immediately.

"Simon, I believe he has something that belongs to you," Monty said. "It would be appreciated if you could take your blade back."

"On it," I said, extending a hand. Ebonsoul turned to silver mist and raced over to me, reforming in my hand. "This is *my* blade."

"I see I'm going to have to kill you all," Gwell said, looking down at his empty hand. "A minor inconvenience, to acquire that which is rightfully mine."

"You should have stayed dead," Monty said, reaching behind him and drawing the Sorrows. They wailed as he entered an offensive stance, and I was immediately creeped out, because they sounded like the soulless when they shrieked, only with less agony and more sadness. "Now, I will have to end you...again."

Gwell formed a cloud of soulless around his hand. With his other hand, he gestured and solidified the soulless into a blade of living darkness.

"A soulless blade is not fair," I said, closing the distance. "How is he even still connected to them?"

"An excellent question," Monty said as he parried a thrust and side stepped a slash as Gwell tried to bisect him. "There must still be a conduit to the soulless."

Gwell formed several black orbs and unleashed them. I parried one with Ebonsoul and dodged to the side as the second and third crashed into the wall where I stood, leaving lingering darkness in the holes they created.

"Don't get hit by those orbs," I called out as I dodged again. "They have some extra nastiness to them."

"I noticed," Monty said, deflecting two orbs and slicing through two more as he engaged Gwell. "This is what you wanted. Ever since I was a child, you wanted my death."

"Not just your death," Gwell said, ducking and allowing my hellhound to sail over his head before blinking out again.

"All of the Montagues deserve death! Once I deal with you, your uncle is next."

He was in for a rude awakening if he thought Dexter was going to be an easy fight. Besides, he still had to get past me, Monty, and my hellhound.

"You never amounted to much as a necromancer," Monty said. "That's why my uncle never paid you any attention. You were too scared to face him in a duel. But a child... You were brave enough to trick two children into dying for your cowardice."

"Taylor was a blight on the sect and you and your family should have never been allowed to join in the first place," he snapped. "You were all inferior magic users."

"Inferior to whom? You?" Monty said.

He blocked the soulless blade as several orbs raced at him from his blind spot. I jumped in the air, leading with Ebonsoul, and attempted to intercept them.

I miscalculated the jump and two orbs punched into my chest. I looked down and expected two smoking holes where my chest used to be, but saw no damage. I gave a silent thanks to the Morrigan and made a mental note to thank her for my runed clothing.

I rolled to my feet as Peaches blinked back in and crashed into Gwell, before blinking out again. Gwell flew off and landed hard on his side. He extended a hand and produced a small cloud of soulless, as the runes on my blade glowed a dull white.

"Simon, your blade—it's the conduit," Monty called out. "You need to absorb it."

"But if I absorb it—"

"Now! Simon! Do it!"

I absorbed Ebonsoul and a surge of energy raced into my body, threatening to overwhelm my senses. I fell to one knee as the energy gripped me. Gwell laughed and began a complicated series of gestures.

"Fools," Gwell scoffed. "You have just handed me this battle. I will enjoy seeing you both beg me for—"

"Nothing," Monty said, releasing a green teleportation circle—this one was mixed with violet-and-black symbols—which slammed into Gwell's chest. "It's over."

"Over?" Gwell said. "Nothing is over! I am Gwell, the Master Necromancer! You cannot defeat me!"

The circle that impacted his chest spread until it covered his entire torso. Monty walked over to where Gwell stood and gestured, forming a golden restraining lattice around him.

"You can't hold me," Gwell continued and gestured, sending black orbs against the lattice. "This paltry cast is nothing against my power. I will kill you, Montague."

"No. No, you won't," Monty said. "Simon, form your weapon."

"You want me to form it now?"

"Yes. The soulless need rest," Monty said. "Gwell has kept them in stasis for too long. They deserve peace." He glanced at Taylor. "They all do."

I formed Ebonsoul.

A cloud of soulless exploded out of my blade and hovered in the air near me. For a few seconds, I thought Monty had miscalculated, but the soulless swayed in the air and then homed in on Gwell.

"No," Gwell said, fear lacing his voice. "Stay away! You stay away from me!"

The cloud zeroed in on the teleportation circle that covered Gwell's torso. They slammed into him but disappeared as they hit him.

He was acting as a portal for the soulless.

He slowly became less solid and started becoming transparent.

"What's happening to him?" I asked. "It looks like—"

"The soulless are devouring his life-force and returning to where they belong," Monty said. "He ripped them from their dimension and utilized them as a weapon. They are undoing that act."

"They're sentient?"

"Sentient is too strong a word; *aware* would be closer to their state of being," Monty as he stepped closer to Gwell. "You won't be returning from this. There is no tether for you to use and Taylor will cease being a shadewalker. You are finished."

"You deserve to die a hundred times over, Montague," Gwell spat. "You and your family are lower than filth. I will see you broken and destroyed. These scars will be with you as long as you draw breath."

"For my acts, yes, I do deserve death many times over," Monty said, his voice serious as he headed over to where Taylor stood. "I am a battle mage. I am not proud of all the things I have done in my life. Yes, I have taken lives"—he glanced at Taylor—"and at times doing so has been a grave error. I cannot undo what has been done. I can only strive to live a life that honors those who wrongfully fell by my hand."

"Pretty words will not save you, Montague," Gwell said. "You will be cursed for as long as you—"

Monty made a fist and the teleportation circle, now filled with soulless, expanded and enveloped Gwell.

He was gone a moment later.

"I never said I was looking for salvation," Monty said, mostly to himself, before turning to Taylor. "I am truly sorry, Taylor."

"It's irreversible, isn't it?"

"I'm afraid so," Monty said as the darkness around the golden lattice grew in size. "I have to sever the tether holding you here or I will doom you to a non-existence of roaming the shores of oblivion."

"Is that where Gwell went?" Taylor asked. "I hope he suffers."

"Rest assured that wherever he goes, he will suffer every moment, knowing he is not here, living the life he had grasped in his hands and stolen from you."

"Good," Taylor whispered. "I do apologize, Tristan. I hope one day you can forgive me."

"I am the one who needs to be forgiven," Monty said heavily. "I should have been a better friend to you. I should have been there for you. I let my ego get in the way, and it cost you your life."

"Your ego was only slightly smaller than mine," Taylor said with a small smile. "Don't blame yourself."

Monty shook his head, his eyes down. "I should have seen Gwell's machinations. I should have seen his hand in this."

"There was no way you could have," Taylor said quietly, looking from Monty to me. "I bear you no ill will. We were both young, our heads full of grandiose ideas, most of them petty and foolish."

"We could have been good friends."

"Don't squander the friendship you have now," Taylor said. "You two have a strong bond. You're family."

Monty nodded, looking away before taking a deep breath and looking back at Taylor.

"Are you ready?"

Taylor nodded.

"Before you send me on my way, does the Golden Circle still exist?"

"In a manner of speaking, yes," Monty said. "If you would believe it, my uncle is running it as a school now."

"Dexter? The head of a school? I almost feel sorry for

those students," Taylor said with a small laugh. "May I make one last request?"

"Of course."

"Could you make sure my family name is remembered in some way in the Golden Circle? My family always hoped I would create a legacy for the Taylor name."

"I'll make sure it's done," Monty said. "Goodbye, Taylor."

"Goodbye, Montague," Taylor said. "It was good to see you again, if only briefly."

"You as well."

Monty gestured and the golden tether appeared again, but this time it began to disintegrate slowly, starting at Monty and ending at Taylor. When it was completely gone, so was Taylor.

"He's gone?" I asked. "For real?"

"We traveled his road to the end," Monty said. "He's gone for real."

"Is Gwell really suffering?"

"I don't know," Monty said. "I've never died, remained a shadewalker, only to be dispatched with soulless. I'd say you would know more on that subject than I."

"I've never been a shadewalker, and I've never even seen the soulless before now," I said, looking down the street at the Dark Goat still lying on its side. "I hope I never see them again."

"Neither do I," Monty said, pulling out his phone. "Cecil will not be pleased the Dark Goat survived this encounter."

"I'm sure he will enjoy hearing that his runework survived the soulless," I said. "How do you even test for something like that? Do I even want to know?"

"Probably not," Monty said, forming a large sausage and feeding it to my hellhound who'd blinked in a second before. "He is a mighty good boy."

I watched my ever-voracious hellhound suction in the sausage and laughed as I tugged on his neck.

"He certainly is," I said, heading over to the Dark Goat with Monty and a semi-satisfied hellhound next to me. "Make the call. Let's go home."

TWENTY-EIGHT

NEW YORK CITY ABANDONED SUBWAY STATION
18TH STREET

"Out of all the places we could have met, you chose this place?" Dira asked, looking around the dim graffiti-filled station. "Why?"

"It's hidden in plain sight," the hooded figure said. "Do you agree to our terms?"

"I'm here."

"True I just need to make sure," the hooded figure said. "Your hand, please. The Order has protocols."

Dira extended a hand.

With an imperceptible cut, in one smooth move, the hooded figure drew a blade and ran it across her hand, before doing the same to Dira. She sheathed her blade and extended her hand to Dira, who clasped it, joining the wounds in a bloody handshake.

The wounds healed seconds later.

"Can you do it?" Dira asked. "I only ask because—"

"I only have one arm?" the hooded figure said. "I am more

effective now with one arm, than I ever was with two. Do you truly want the Mark?"

"Yes, more than breath itself," Dira said. "Do you have the weapon?"

"Yes, with this blade you will command the assistance you need." The hooded figured reached back, grabbed a rune-covered sheath, and handed it to Dira. "Handle that with the utmost care. There are few left in the world."

Dira took the sheath and held it with reverence.

"I only need to deal with this Director Nakatomi, and you will assist me with my...difficulty?"

"Yes, we are familiar with Strong," the hooded figure answered, unconsciously rubbing her shoulder. "That blade should prove effective against the Director *and* Strong."

"The enemy of my enemy is my friend," Dira said, drawing the black blade from the sheath and admiring it. "A true kamikira."

"By the time we are done, the vampires will be running for their lives, and you will be the new Marked of Kali," the hooded figure said. "To alliances of death."

"To alliances of death," Dira said, sheathing the blade again.

THE END

AUTHOR NOTES

Thank you for reading this story and jumping into the world of Monty & Strong with me.

Disclaimer: The Author Notes are written at the very end of the writing process. This section is not seen by the ART or my amazing Jeditor—Audrey. Any typos or errors following this disclaimer are mine and mine alone.

This one was both easy and hard to write.

There were parts where I really had to push to get the ideas across and there were parts where it was a typical M&S story, flowing easily.

First, before anything else, thank you for joining me on this insane adventure! This is M&S Book 22, and my brain boggles at that concept, it truly is awe-inspiring. I didn't anticipate writing this book so fast. The story was ready to be written if that made any sense, I won't say how fast this book was written, but it was faster than Peaches inhales a sausage when he's hungry, and he's *always* hungry lol.

I understand that the concept of a corpse road may still be hard to define for some. In the context of this book, it's traveling down a path to reconcile something in your past that you have been reluctant to face. Something you know you need to face and put to rest permanently (like a corpse?).

For Monty, it was his time as a battle mage and his early years in the Golden Circle. There were many things he opted to just turn his back on. Many times this happens in our lives because it's too painful to face the reality of our past actions. In many cases, the wounds are still fresh even after many years have past.

Sometimes, its because we haven't forgiven ourselves and feel we deserve to be punished for the acts we committed, that, in our eyes, are heinous and unforgivable.

We are our own harshest critics. Monty still has a lot to process, learning to let go of the anger and rage isa step in the right direction.

This story was Monty going through that in a way only a mage like him can. There are many more wounds he needs to explore (Simon too), but I'll try not to get too dark and dour. After all, Monty will have to face the shadows of his past to grow as a mage on this new path he's on. It will be painful and difficult, but he will be able to face these difficulties, because he's not alone—he has Simon, and Peaches...and us.

It was interesting to see how polarizing Anu was in this story. I won't go into too much detail. He is a complex character who will return in the future books. There is so much to him that has not been revealed that will be. We don't know everything about him and Kengir, but we will revisit and explore more and more will be explained. You know how this goes by now, don't you?

I was of two minds on the ending of this book with the preview of IMMORTAL which is the next book. Part of me wanted to end on Chapter 27, but I felt that it was important to include Chapter 28 and the reveal of the conversation of Dira and the one armed (not so mysterious) hooded figure.

Let me know your thoughts on it. I can promise you one thing , there is no way you are going to be able to see what's coming for MS&P in the next book.

Things are going to get deadly in a hurry and they are not ready.

They are so not ready.

I only have one word for you—crossbows.

Th next book (that is not M&S) will be ENDGAME TANGO to close out the trilogy for Treadwell. That story promises to be a rollercoaster for Sebastian and crew. Regina will be unleashed and she is going to use Maledicta to further her own plans. She doesn't care what Cinder or Char say, she's going to do her own thing and if that means setting the city on fire and watching it burn, well, she has an extra pack of marshmallows and is ready for the bonfire.

Does she have serious issues? Yes...yes she does.

Is she dangerous and unhinged?

I would say she's on the edge, but she's so far past the edge, that we can't even see the edge any longer. Even with all that, she still has a soft spot for Sebastian, its just everyone else that she wants to eliminate.

There will be some huge ups and down in the next few M&S books, there will be plenty of surprises and moments where you will want to hunt me down. I apologize now, beforehand, but these things need to happen.

What else can I say?

I really enjoyed creating this story for you. It was different, slightly odd, and hard to understand, but a part of me feels that this is the kind of story that needs to be read a few times to really be understood.

It's like an onion...layers and layers.

I have a few dark and spicy ideas percolating in my brain. I may soon create a serial of episodic stores with Simon as the Morrigan's Man. A look to the time when he starts to fulfill his obligation to Badb Catha. It's still in the idea phase, but the conversation in this book between Simon and Mo, really got me thinking about how to bring that story to you. Like I said still in the idea phase...we will see.

As always, I couldn't do this incredibly insane adventure without you, my amazing reader. You jump into these adventures with me, when I say "WHAT IF?" you say: "Hmmm what if indeed. Let's find out where that idea goes!"

For that, I humbly and deeply thank you.

I consider myself deeply fortunate to have a MoB Family that is willing to jump into these worlds with the same abandon I have in writing them. I have always said that I have the most amazing readers on the planet. This is actually true and documented, I just verified it this moment, and if it's written here, it MUST be true.

On a side note, BLUR is being worked on for its rerelease TBA soon™! Not only is BLUR coming out again, but the rest of the series is being worked on as well. Once I know more about John Kane and his world, I will share it with you.

I want you to know that I am deeply honored that you would join me in the creations of my semi-twisted imagination as we drive, fly, and explode our way through the worlds of my mind. What are you thinking? This is dangerous stuff we are doing, living out on the edge of the imagination and letting the products of a caffeine soaked brain loose on an unsuspecting world.

They are not ready lol!

So how do we get ready?

Load up the extra large thermos with Death Wish (extra-extra), slide into the Dark Goat (don't worry it gets fixed after this book. Gently shove the creature vaguely resembling a canine to one side, if he lets you. I hear pastrami is good for getting him to move. Two large bowls might help.), strap in tight and hold on.

We have plans to foil, people to save, and property to destroy!

In the immortal sage words of our resident Zen Hellhound Master...

Meat is Life!

Thank you again for jumping into this story with me!

BITTEN PEACHES PUBLISHING

<u>Thanks for Reading!</u>
If you enjoyed this book, would you please **leave a review** at
the site you purchased it from? It doesn't have to be long...
just a line or two would be fantastic and it would really help
me out.

<u>Bitten Peaches Publishing **offers more books and audiobooks**</u>
across various genres including: urban fantasy, science fiction,
adventure, & mystery!

www.BittenPeachesPublishing.com

<u>More books by Orlando A. Sanchez</u>

<u>Montague & Strong Detective Agency Novels</u>
Tombyards & Butterflies•Full Moon Howl•Blood is
Thicker•Silver Clouds Dirty Sky•Homecoming•Dragons &
Demigods•Bullets & Blades•Hell Hath No Fury•Reaping
Wind•The Golem•Dark Glass•Walking the

Razor•Requiem•Divine Intervention•Storm
Blood•Revenant•Blood Lessons•Broken Magic•Lost
Runes•Archmage•Entropy•Corpse Road

Montague & Strong Detective Agency Stories
No God is Safe•The Date•The War Mage•A Proper
Hellhound•The Perfect Cup•Saving Mr. K

Night Warden Novels
Wander•ShadowStrut•Nocturne Melody

Rule of the Council
Blood Ascension•Blood Betrayal•Blood Rule

The Warriors of the Way
The Karashihan•The Spiritual Warriors•The Ascendants•The
Fallen Warrior•The Warrior Ascendant•The Master Warrior

John Kane
The Deepest Cut•Blur

Sepia Blue
The Last Dance•Rise of the Night•Sisters•Night-
mare•Nameless•Demon

Chronicles of the Modern Mystics
The Dark Flame•A Dream of Ashes

The Treadwell Supernatural Directive
The Stray Dogs•Shadow Queen

Brew & Chew Adventures
Hellhound Blues

Bangers & Mash
Bangers & Mash

Tales of the Gatekeepers
Bullet Ballet•The Way of Bug•Blood Bond

Division 13
The Operative•The Magekiller

Blackjack Chronicles
The Dread Warlock

The Assassin's Apprentice
The Birth of Death

Gideon Shepherd Thrillers
Sheepdog

DAMNED
Aftermath

Nyxia White
They Bite•They Rend•They Kill

Iker the Cleaner
Iker the Unseen•Daystrider•Nightwalker

Stay up to date with new releases!
Shop www.orlandoasanchez.com for more books and
audiobooks!

CONTACT ME

To send me a message, email me at:
orlando@orlandoasanchez.com

Join our newsletter:
www.orlandoasanchez.com

Stay up to date with new releases and audiobooks!
Shop: www.orlandoasanchez.com

For more information on the M&S World...come join the
MoB Family on Facebook!
You can find us at:
<u>Montague & Strong Case Files</u>

Visit our online M&S World Swag Store located at:
<u>Emandes</u>

For exclusive stories...join our Patreon!
Patreon

Please follow our amazing instagram page at:
bittenpeaches

Follow us on Youtube:
Bitten Peaches Publishing Storyteller

If you enjoyed the book, **please leave a review**. Reviews help the book, and also help other readers find good stories to read.

<u>THANK YOU!</u>

ART SHREDDERS

I want to take a moment to extend a special thanks to the ART SHREDDERS.

No book is the work of one person. I am fortunate enough to have an amazing team of advance readers and shredders.

Thank you for giving of your time and keen eyes to provide notes, insights, answers to the questions, and corrections (dealing wonderfully with my extreme dreaded comma allergy). You help make every book and story go from good to great. Each and every one of you helped make this book fantastic, and I couldn't do this without each of you.

THANK YOU

<u>ART SHREDDERS</u>

Amber, Anne Morando, Audrey Cienki, Avon Perry
    Beverly Collie
    Cat, Chris Christman II

Daniel Parr, Diane Craig, Dolly Sanchez, Donna Young Hatridge

Hal Bass, Helen

James Wheat, Jasmine Breeden, Jasmine Davis, Jeanette Auer, Jen Cooper, Joy Kiili, Julie Peckett

Karen Hollyhead

Larry Diaz Tushman, Laura Tallman I, Luann Zipp

Malcolm Robertson, Marcia Campbell, Maryelaine Eckerle-Foster, Melissa Miller, Melody DeLoach, Michelle Blue

Paige Guido

RC Battels, Rene Corrie, Rob Farnham, Rohan Gandhy

Sondra Massey, Stacey Stein, Susie Johnson

Tami Cowles, Ted Camer, Terri Adkisson

Vikki Brannagan

Wendy Schindler

PATREON SUPPORTERS

TO ALL OUR PATRONS

I want to extend a special note of gratitude to all of our
Patrons in
The Magick Squad.

Your generous support helps me to continue on this amazing
adventure called 'being an author'.
I deeply and truly appreciate each of you for your selfless act
of patronage.

You are all amazing beyond belief.
***
If you are not a patron, and would like to enjoy the exclusive
stories available only to our members...join the Squad!

The Magick Squad

THANK YOU

Alisha Harper, Amber Dawn Sessler, Angela Tapping, Anne Morando, Anthony Hudson, Ashley Britt

Brenda French

Carl Skoll, Carrie O'Leary, Cat Inglis, Chad Bowden, Chris Christman II, Cindy Deporter, Connie Cleary

David Smith, Dan Fong, Davis Johnson, Diane Garcia, Diane Jackson, Diane Kassmann, Dorothy Phillips

Elizabeth Barbs, Enid Rodriguez, Eric Maldonato, Eve Bartlet, Ewan Mollison

Federica De Dominicis, Fluff Chick Productions, Francis August Valanzola

Gail Ketcham Hermann, Gary McVicar, Geoff Siegel, Grace Gemeinhardt, Groove72

Heidi Wolfe

Ingrid Schijven

Jacob Anderson, James Wheat, Jannine Zerres, Jasmine Breeden, Jeffrey Juchau, Jim Maguire, Jo Dungey, Joe Durham, John Fauver, Joy Kiili, Joy T, Just Jeanette

Kathy Ringo, Kimberly Curington, Krista Fox

Leona Jackson, Lisa Simpson, Lizzette Piltch

Malcolm Robertson, Mark Morgan, Mary Barzee, Mary Beth Wright, Marydot Pinto, Maureen McCallan, Mel Brown, Melissa Miller, Meri, Duncanson

Paige Guido, Patricia Pearson, Patrick Gregg

Ralph Kroll, Renee Penn, Robert Walters

Sammy Dawkins, Sara M Branson, Sara N Morgan, Sarah Sofianos, Sassy Bear, Sharon Elliott, Shelby, Sonyia Roy, Stacey Stein, Steven Huber, Susan Spry

Tami Cowles, Terri Adkisson, Tommy

Van Nebedum

Wanda Corder-Jones, Wendy Schindler

ACKNOWLEDGEMENTS

With each book, I realize that every time I learn something about this craft, it highlights so many things I still have to learn. Each book, each creative expression, has a large group of people behind it.

This book is no different.

Even though you see one name on the cover, it is with the knowledge that I am standing on the shoulders of the literary giants that informed my youth, and am supported by my generous readers who give of their time to jump into the adventures of my overactive imagination.

I would like to take a moment to express my most sincere thanks:

To Dolly: My wife and greatest support. You make all this possible each and every day. You keep me grounded when I get lost in the forest of ideas. Thank you for asking the right questions when needed, and listening intently when I go off on tangents. Thank you for who you are and the space you create—I love you.

To my Tribe: You are the reason I have stories to tell. You cannot possibly fathom how much and how deeply I love you all.

To Lee: Because you were the first audience I ever had. I love you, sis.

To the Logsdon Family: The words *thank you* are insufficient to describe the gratitude in my heart for each of you. JL, your support always demands I bring my best, my A-game, and produce the best story I can. Both you and Lorelei (my Uber Jeditor) and now, Audrey, are the reason I am where I am today.

It is with some sadness, that I want to acknowledge, and express my deepest gratitude to my editor, Audrey, who is stepping away from her editing adventures. I wish you all the best in the next chapter of your life, whatever that may be. May your next adventure be more amazing than this one. I know that whatever you take on, you will excel at it.

Thank you for the notes, challenges, corrections, advice, and laughter. Your patience is truly infinite. *Arigatogozaimasu.*

To The Montague & Strong Case Files Group—AKA The MoB (Mages of Badassery): When I wrote T&B there were fifty-five members in The MoB. As of this release, there are over one thousand five hundred members in the MoB. I am honored to be able to call you my MoB Family. Thank you for being part of this group and M&S.

You make this possible. **THANK YOU.**

To the ever-vigilant PACK: You help make the MoB...the MoB. Keeping it a safe place for us to share and just...be.

Thank you for your selfless vigilance. You truly are the Sentries of Sanity.

Chris Christman II: A real-life technomancer who makes the **MoBTV LIVEvents +Kaffeeklatsch** on YouTube amazing. Thank you for your tireless work and wisdom. Everything is connected...you totally rock!

To the WTA—The Incorrigibles: JL, Ben Z., Eric QK., S.S., and Noah.

They sound like a bunch of badass misfits, because they are. My exposure to the deranged and deviant brain trust you all represent helped me be the author I am today. I have officially gone to the *dark side* thanks to all of you. I humbly give you my thanks, and...it's all your fault.

To my fellow Indie Authors: I want to thank each of you for creating a space where authors can feel listened to, and encouraged to continue on this path. A rising tide lifts all the ships indeed.

To The English Advisory: Aaron, Penny, Carrie, Davina, and all of the UK MoB. For all things English...thank you.

To DEATH WISH COFFEE: This book (and every book I write) has been fueled by generous amounts of the only coffee on the planet (and in space) strong enough to power my very twisted imagination. Is there any other coffee that can compare? I think not. DEATH WISH—thank you!

To Deranged Doctor Design: Kim, Darja, Tanja, Jovana, and Milo (Designer Extraordinaire).

If you've seen the covers of my books and been amazed, you can thank the very talented and gifted creative team at

DDD. They take the rough ideas I give them, and produce incredible covers that continue to surprise and amaze me. Each time, I find myself striving to write a story worthy of the covers they produce. DDD, you embody professionalism and creativity. Thank you for the great service and spectacular covers. **YOU GUYS RULE!**

To you, the reader: I was always taught to save the best for last. I write these stories for **you**. Thank you for jumping down the rabbit holes of *what if?* with me. You are the reason I write the stories I do.

You keep reading...I'll keep writing.

Thank you for your support and encouragement.

SPECIAL MENTIONS

To Dolly: my rock, anchor, and inspiration. Thank you...always.

Larry & Tammy—The WOUF: Because even when you aren't there...you're there.

Orlando A. Sanchez
www.orlandoasanchez.com

Orlando has been writing ever since his teens when he was immersed in creating scenarios for playing Dungeons and Dragons with his friends every weekend.

The worlds of his books are urban settings with a twist of the paranormal lurking just behind the scenes and with generous doses of magic, martial arts, and mayhem.

He currently resides in Queens, NY with his wife and children.

Thanks for Reading!

If you enjoyed this book, would you **please leave a review** at the site you purchased it from? It doesn't have to be a book report... just a line or two would be fantastic and it would really help us out!

Printed in Great Britain
by Amazon

38510142R10142